Gaby Triana

RIDING THE UNIVERSE

HARPER TEEN

An Imprint of HarperCollinsPublishers

HarperTeen is an imprint of HarperCollins Publishers.

www.harperteen.com

Library of Congress Cataloging-in-Publication Data
Triana, Gaby.
  Riding the universe / Gaby Triana. — 1st ed.
    p. cm.
  Summary: Seventeen-year-old Chloé, who inherited her uncle's
beloved Harley after his death, spends the subsequent year trying to pass
chemistry, wondering whether she should look for her birth parents, and
beginning an unlikely relationship with her chemistry tutor, while also
trying to figure out how she really feels about the boy who has been her
best friend since they were children.
  ISBN 978-0-06-088570-0 (trade bdg.)
  [1. Grief—Fiction. 2. Dating (Social customs)—Fiction. 3. Uncles—
Fiction. 4. Adoption—Fiction. 5. Motorcycles—Fiction. 6. Interpersonal
relations—Fiction. 7. High schools—Fiction. 8. Schools—Fiction.
9. Florida—Fiction.] I. Title.
PZ7.T7334Ri 2009   2008031451
[Fic]—dc22   CIP
                                                                 AC

Typography by Joel Tippie
09 10 11 12 13   LP/RRDB   10 9 8 7 6 5 4 3 2 1
❖
First Edition

For Chris

Prologue

Her black body, blue airbrushed flames, and sloping ape hangers reflect the dim light of our garage. A single drop of oil drips onto the concrete floor where she stands cooling off. My uncle's voice resonates in my mind. *We built her, Chlo. You and me. Now you know the hard work that goes into one of these babies.*

I look at my father, who sits on a stool, sorting stuff to keep from stuff to throw out. His brown eyes have a permanent squint from the ocean's glare. His skin is bronzed from long days in the sun, his shirt stained with fish guts. Normally, he would sympathize with my life's plight and purpose. He would go easy on me whenever I slip up. Not today. Today, his parent hat is on. Lucky me.

"Pull that grade up to at least a C, *o no mas* Lolita." He leans forward on his stool, elbows on his knees. I can see how hard this is for him. He knows how much I love Lolita and the effect this is having on me. He may not be my real dad, but he knows me better than any biological father could. "Mom and I only let you ride her because of your promise, but you're not passing chemistry. And a deal is a deal. Are you listening, *linda*?"

My eyes shift back to my Harley-Davidson 1200 Sportster. I try to picture life without her, imagine her gone, like my uncle Seth, but I just can't. Because it's not going to happen. Because I must not, no matter what, lose her.

"Chloé?" he demands.

Lolita's engine ticks as she cools off. We have a lot in common, she and I.

"Yes, Papi." I grit my teeth. "I know. I'll bring up my grade."

One

The stars are out. All 100 billion of them in our galaxy alone. I can't see them this lovely January morning at 7:35 A.M., but I know they're there. Same way they have been for 13 billion years.

The closest one to Earth is particularly bright today. I wish I could go to the dock and bask in the sun's glow this morning, but I can't. Because today is the day I deal with my knowledge deficiency head-on. If I don't, well . . . my father has made it clear what will happen.

So instead, I lock the front door, kick the porch swing to wake up Rock Nuñez, my loitering best friend who waits there for me in the mornings, and head to the open garage. "Ready to lose?" I ask.

"Okay, doll. Whatever you say," he grunts, rolling over to stretch. He picks up the lemon-poppy muffin my mom has left for him on the bench and eats half of it in one bite. Then he stands, ruffles his hair, and heads to his car—a '68 suped-up black Ford Mustang parked on the curb. If I ever wanted to drive a car instead of a motorcycle, that'd be the one.

I pull on my helmet, close the garage door, then start Lolita. Her loud engine and pipes replace the morning silence. The Mustang roars to life, and minutes later, we're off and racing—the perfect start to our day.

We fly past palmettos and new home developments, wind charging at us at seventy miles an hour. He passes me. I pass him. The cars on the road keep to the right. They know better than to get in our way. My braid bangs against my back, my arms vibrate with glee. I grip Lolita's accelerator and punch it as far as it'll go, and she presses on with happy speed. I blow past Rock, singing into the wind. "Woooo!"

This is life. This is how I want to die.

But not today. Obviously.

It's our first day back from winter break, and I have made Papi a promise to be more academically responsible. So, as much as I want to race around town with Rock all morning, I slow down and cruise to the next exit. He swings into line behind me. Our morning chase has come to a close, and once again I am victorious. All hail Chloé, Queen of Harleys!

As much as I love riding Lolita, it has one huge downside. She's only mine because Seth's not here anymore. My uncle left this planet five months and nineteen days ago, so now the bike belongs to me. Considering I helped give her new life seven years ago through blood, sweat, and motor oil—our little summer project when I was ten—my parents figure that's how he would've wanted it.

But I'd give her back in a heartbeat to have him here again.

On the last overpass, I see my destination in the distance. Everglades High, HOME OF THE CROCS *(croc of crap, croc of shit)*! When the light turns green, I lunge out of first. Lolita protests with a cough. *I know, chica, tune-up coming soon. Sigh.*

My first class of the day is the one I'm failing—Basic Chemistry. It's bad enough my brain has a hard time understanding mols, elements, and ions, but the school board made things infinitely worse by having Mr. Rooney, a living mummy and the Eighth Wonder of the Ancient World, teach it with his outdated methods and complete lack of connection with modern-day students. Mr. Rooney, by the way, will be closing his classroom in exactly three minutes, regardless of who is making out in the doorway.

I hurry to 147th Avenue, Rock following close behind me like my dance partner in a highly choreographed ballet. We enter the student parking lot. My assigned space awaits. A student here at 'Glades High whose name I won't mention (Philip Best) complained that my motorcycle needn't take up one entire "car" space best reserved for higher-order motor vehicles, so the office gave me a "special" parking space for my "special" vehicle. It may be an entire astronomical unit (93 million miles) from the entrance to the school, but I smile and do as I'm asked.

Today is a new day! I remind myself.

I park, cut the engine, and lock up. I hate not being able to monitor Lolita from Rooney's window, but Principal Dunnar doesn't care. He doesn't understand that a motorcycle is not a car or a truck. It's more delicate. People like to touch it. But it's still a non-issue for him. As he puts it, "A seventeen-year-old young lady should not be tinkering with dangerous road toys best left for middle-aged men named Hellcat anyway."

Rock jumps out of his car and locks up. He slings his backpack over his shoulder, but I know there's nothing in there except for a few condoms and his phone. "Later, doll." He waves. "I let you win!"

"You wish!" I have one minute and forty-eight seconds until Mr. Rooney slams his door, sits at his desk, and starts talking to his grade book. "Later, Lola," I address her the way Seth used to. Cradling my helmet, I break into a fast walk. I'm releasing my hair from its braid and taking off my shades when I hear it—the electronic whine of the first-period bell. *Damn it.*

I try to hurry without running. Running would attract more attention. Oh, look, it's Philip Best in the hall. I do everything in my power not to hiss at him. What did he care if I was taking up a Whole Entire Parking Spot? Am I not a Whole Entire Student? *Ha, ha, your car is blocked by Rock's.* I smile at him. He returns it with a wary glare.

"Chloé Rodriguez!" A beautiful, accented voice echoes behind me in the first hallway. My *marraine* (godmother), Colette Jordan, peers out of her French classroom as if the wall has grown a head. "I do not mark you present every morning for you to walk all over my generosity with your tardiness, *comprennez?*"

"*Oui*, Madame Jordan." I was lucky enough to land Marraine for homeroom this year. Her act of kindness each morning affords me an extra eight minutes of sleep. "It won't happen again."

"No. It won't. And tell your mother I'll be there tonight."

"I will. *Merci,* Madame. *Tu es un ange!*"

She *humphs* and disappears into her classroom. *Whew.* It is with mixed emotions that I attend the very school where my mother's best friend (aka reconnaissance spy) also happens to teach. Of all the high schools in Florida City. Okay it's the only high school in Florida City.

"Hey, Chloé." A blur resembling Vincent Maroone whooshes past me.

"'Sup, Vince."

"I'm working at Gears Auto now, did you hear?" He turns around and walks backward. I know he's trying his best to act bad-ass, but all I see is the doofy twelve-year-old who crushed on me for three years in middle school.

"Awesome. Free oil for me."

"You know it." The cigarette he has tucked behind his ear falls, and he has to stop and get it, breaking his ultracool momentum.

"Smoking is bad for you, Vincent."

"Yeah, it makes you late." He does a weird two-finger salute, then takes off running again. Our security guard appears from around a corner and tells him to slow down.

I hurry for the stairs. When I round the corner, I run smack into Gordon Spoo . . . Spoo *something.* I can never remember. Spoonbill? Tall guy, a little chunky, but cute.

Sort of full of himself, which I have always found strangely attractive. He used to go out with co-Mensa genius, Sabine Jimenez, at the beginning of the school year.

"Sorry about that," I say, looking for a way around him.

He blocks me like the Wall of China that he is. "Late again?"

Quoi? Who is he, my parole officer? "I was just . . . it's that I was in . . ." *Find yourself, Chloé.* "Move," I tell him.

He steps aside to let me pass, then smirks. "Hurry up, or you'll be late to Rooney's," he says like he's my *mom*, then adds, "Motor Girl."

Nice. I see he has employed the nickname other students have adopted for me because they think they are witty and referential. For all I know, he may be really nice once I get to know him, but right now, I don't plan on it. I push past him, then realize he has uttered something more important than my pet name. I stop and turn around. "How do you know what class . . . ?"

But Gordon is gone. And oddly, so is my breath.

No time to think about this now.

Ancient Rooney's class awaits, right across from the stairwell. Looks like I'm the only one arriving late this morning. Fabulous. As punishment, I'll have to recite the periodic chart in ascending order by group, starting with the noble gases—a skill I'm unlikely to use ever again.

When I open the door quietly, Mr. Rooney has his nose inside his grade book like he expects it to speak. *Shh, listen.* It tells Mr. Rooney something of the utmost importance. Ah, yes, he has entered an *A* in it and must quickly revoke it before anyone actually passes his class. I sneak in as quietly as humanly possible while my classmates look on in amusement. I nod at my friends Pedro and Alejandra (or PedAndra, as I like to call them) and tiptoe to a window seat in the third row.

"Chloé!" Mr. Rooney croaks suddenly. I am not kidding. Picture a frog, and the frog says "Chloé."

"Yes?" I smile, thinking up a quick excuse. *You see, there was an accident on the Turnpike, Mr. Rooney, and it was quite the doozie.* Mr. Rooney would understand a word like *doozie.* But then I notice Pedro shaking his head at me, because what idiot would say "yes?" during roll call?

"I mean, here." I bite my lip. *Please, don't make me stand up. Oh, God . . . argon, helium, xenon . . .*

Mr. Rooney tries focusing on me, but I'm too far away for his olden little eyes, so he goes back to calling roll, one name per minute. *Yes!* I slip my chem book out of my backpack and let out a huge, slow breath. I will not be reciting the noble gases after all.

Around me, other students finish winter-break home-work, checking the back of the book for answers. Which reminds me. I take out my notebook and get started. I know nothing about chemistry, other than what happens when baking soda reacts with vinegar. I am so toast.

Today, Mr. Rooney wears his lime green lab coat, because he is a *hip* old mummy. I'd rather watch my mother hang underwear on a clothesline and hear her explain how it'll acquire a fresh-baked scent only the sun's life energy can provide, even though we are the proud owners of a fully functioning clothes dryer, than suffer the next fifty minutes. But then I remember I am a prisoner here.

I do my best to focus on the equations in the book, settling my head against my fists—a position that I hope fools Mr. Rooney into thinking I am submerged in the wonders of science. But within minutes, I drift into my first nap of the morning.

Two

I'm riding along Cancún's highway, headed to meet my birth parents. The air is hot and dusty. Suddenly, I see a refreshing blue lagoon up ahead. I stop for a drink of water, and there, waiting for me under a gushing waterfall, is my yummy-cocoa-butter-and-ripped-muscle-y peer tutor, Julio.

"*Bienvenida, mi amor,*" says Julio. I am surprised to see him. My riding jacket and jeans melt away to reveal a teeny bikini.

"Did I keep you waiting long?" I blow him a sexy kiss.

"For you, I wait forever. Ready for your first lesson?" He raises his dark eyebrows and crosses his arms to show off his biceps. The words *stupendous* and *spectacular* separately cannot handle these babies—these are *stupendicular*.

I feel like I am drooling, because . . . I am. The sound of backpacks zipping up has roused me from my last nap of the day at 'Glades High. I wipe my mouth and shake off the dream. Two minutes to the final bell. My zombie classmates and I have reached dismissal without falling off our chairs unconscious. Five months until summer. Why haven't any quantum physicists discovered the secret to time-leaping yet?

Outside, the sky has turned gray. Lolita will definitely get rained on, but I can't rescue her right now: Peer tutoring awaits. My stomach hurts. I've never had a peer tutor before. I can already tell I'm not going to like it. What's to like about someone your age, or even younger than you, knowing you're a dumb-ass? I pray to the gods of Afterschool Academics that my tutor is not Sabine. Because to get Sabine would Sa-suck. Sabine is a cross between a girl and a gargoyle—a *girlgoyle*.

Then I see Rock down the hall. He jogs up and crushes his sculptured arms around me. "Chloeeee!" he cheers. He's rather strong for a best friend, but I am too. I elbow him hard.

He recoils like a wounded snake. "Ow! What was that for?"

"Where were you at lunch?" I ask. "Dead somewhere?"

"Nah, you can't kill a bad weed, sweetheart."

"True, but you've been spending less and less time with me. If you're not careful, I may get jealous." I wink at him.

"You? Jealous?" He laughs. "Now that's funny. Listen, Chlo, I gotta talk to you later."

"About?"

"I'll just talk to you later."

"You know where to find me." It's probably about one of his sexquests. I'm tired of doling out free advice.

"Looking good, baby doll." He winks. When he turns around, two senior girls immediately flank him. He puts his arms around their waists, and together they disappear down the hall. The weirdest part is how this kind of thing never seems to bother Amber, his supposed girlfriend. What is *that* relationship all about?

I do have one theory.

Rock was the quietest kid in my third-grade class, the sort of kid who had "Excellent" in conduct but just barely passed all his subjects. One day, he was crying in the playground. When Ms. Morena asked what was wrong, he told her his mother had moved to Kendall with her boyfriend. I heard Ms. M tell him that Kendall wasn't so far away—only forty minutes—but *that* made him cry even more. When she walked away, I sat with him and said that forty minutes must feel like forever and that would probably make me sad too. I'll never forget the long look he gave me. He wiped his nose with his shirt and said, "Wanna race?" We took off running and have been racing ever since.

His dad told him to "man up" and "get over it" lots of times over the years, insisting that he'd still see her whenever he could drive him. But of course, that rarely happened. Since then, Rock and I have taken apart bicycles, motors, and, eventually, whole cars. I've seen him get a few shiners, and I've seen him in his boxers. But I have never seen him without a girl (or two) waiting in the wings. And while I'm no psychotherapist, I have to wonder if he is not somehow trying to replace . . . *Her.*

Freakin' kills me.

After crossing the entire campus, I finally arrive at the auditorium, which is practically *in* the Everglades itself. I almost have to machete my way through cypress trees, pythons, and snapping alligators to get there. I open one of the noisy double doors, and everyone turns to look for a second. At the front of the stage, Ms. Rath and her team of helpful, smart students greet the needy masses. Sabine is among them, reading what appears to be a small 8,995-page book.

I calm my stomach aerobics by taking a few deep breaths. There aren't too many people here, which makes me feel better yet crappier at the same time. I count . . . ten . . . fifteen . . . only twenty kids failing in all of 'Glades? That's impossible. I mean, at lunch today, I ran into a dude ramming his body into the Coke machine that read OUT OF ORDER. Where is *he*?

Ms. Rath flags me down. "Over here, please."

I make my way down the aisle and stop in front of the table.

"Name?"

Ms. Rath reminds me of Gene Simmons, that guy from the old band KISS, but in a dress. Her hair is jet-black and her lips are full, like his.

"Chloé Rodriguez," I mumble, trying not to stare at her manliness.

Sabine looks up at me and smiles with her shiny braces. Forget everything you've ever heard about preachers' daughters being rebellious. This one actually takes after Daddy. Alejandra told me how Sabine gave her the number to AA one time after she saw her sneaking a beer in the parking lot. How did she ever land a boyfriend in the first place? Please don't let me be paired with a girl who thinks she is doing God's work by helping us flawed mortals better themselves.

"You're chemistry, right?" Ms. Rath asks me.

Well, I'm not really chemistry personified, but what did this poor woman ever do to me? I let it slide and smile. "Yes."

"Good, good. Great. Then have a seat with Sabine, sweetheart."

NOOO! I fight the urge to run. So what if I fail Rooney's class? So I won't be a chemist? I never liked Bunsen burners anyway.

Sabine smiles again. It's weird to see a girl my age wearing braces. They completely cover her teeth, so all you see is metal. A smiling, metal-mouthed *girlgoyle*. Help!

"Wanna come this way?"

No.

She gestures at a couple of seats in the second row, where she has already decorated her personal space. There are colored paper clips and colored pens, and I so do not have anything in common with this girl, other than the fact that we are both females who attend the same school. "You're Motor Girl, right?"

Argh.

Yes, I appreciate all things engine and wheels, but when will people stop acting like judgmental dorki and start learning real things about me? Like that I am adopted. Or that I make up new words. That I can point out twenty-five constellations in under two minutes if bribed with a mighty slice of flan. I'm a Wikipedia of astronomical facts, if anyone would bother to notice.

"Chloé," I correct her.

She stutters, "I—I know . . . What I meant was—"

"I know what you meant." I try not to sound snippy, but why shouldn't I be? Have I called her 'Metal-Mouthed Girlgoyle' straight to her face? No, I have not. "It's Chloé."

"Sorry," she says, and actually sounds like she means it. I decide to forgive her right there and stop calling names too. "I'm Sabine."

"Hey, Sabine."

She plops into one of the auditorium seats, which are more like plastic ass-buckets. I sit in the one next to her. I must write the administration a letter thanking them for these butt flatteners. She whips out the same chemistry book that we use in Rooney's class. "I guess we'll start with the structure of atoms. Is that good for you?"

Good for me would be leaving on Lolita and pretending I don't have any failing grades, but since that's not likely to happen . . . "Sure." I take out my notebook and pencil and try to look grateful and interested at the same time. I imagine Sabine as Seth, explaining the difference between chains and belts in older and newer-model Harleys, and before you know it, I'm nodding, jotting things down.

"Sabine?" Ms. Rath hovers above us after about five minutes. "May I see you?"

Sabine sighs and pops up like an Eggo. "Hold on a sec."

The auditorium doors open loudly as someone enters. I look back and see that Gordon dude shaking water off his brown hair and backpack. Great, so it *is* raining. He glances around comfortably. This must be his home turf.

I shrink into my ass-bucket and hide half my face with my hand. *I am not here. I do not need peer tutoring. La, la, la* . . . But then Sabine's back, and I notice her tortured expression when she sees Gordon coming down the aisle. Her eyes look like they're going to explode with tears.

"I'm sorry, Chloé, but she reassigned me," she says, sweeping up her rainbow of paper clips, more than a little frustrated.

"Why?"

"She thinks I'd be better off with—" She points to a girl I recognize as a freshman, wearing little barrettes in her hair. "Francine asked if she could get a girl, and *Gordon* is the only other tutor left." She says *Gordon* like one might say *Lucifer, Ruler of the Underworld.* I'm guessing they did not part on amicable terms.

"Why?" I watch Francine clutching her books tightly. "It's not like she's getting a pap smear."

Sabine shrugs. "Maybe she won't be able to concentrate with him, I don't know . . ." As if Gordon is such a hotbed of orgasmic activity that no one would be able to concentrate around him.

"No problem. Good luck," I say. She smiles back hesitantly before traipsing off, looking back at me and Gordon as if I might start making out with her ex or something. Still, I actually feel disappointed that I came to a truce with Sabine over our nicknames for nothing.

But now this means I'm getting—

"So we meet again, Motor Girl."

17

Three

ordon stares down at me with a look I can only describe as *malevoly*—something both malevolent and "holy moly!"

And I actually thought he might be nice.

But I was wrong.

As I so often am, hence the peer tutoring.

Sabine, come back!

I must remain calm. I can do this.

"Ah, yes. We meet again, Brain Boy." I was going to go with "Mensa Man," but I didn't want him thinking he's a *man* or anything. I notice his shoes are in severe need of updating.

"What are you looking at?" His gaze falls on his feet.

"Nothing."

Gordon's eyebrows draw together. He sits in the plastic ass-bucket next to me. "Sorry I'm late."

"Yes, didn't you chastise me this morning for being late, even though you were too? And look at you now. That's two tardiness strikes." *Score!*

"I wasn't late this morning." He unzips his wet backpack and pulls out a different chemistry book from the one I use. "I was delivering a package to Henley's class."

"Sure you were. And that's not my book."

"I know, but we're going to use it. The other one is obtuse."

Obtuse? Why, I would have said *obtusing* or *obtangle.*

He scribbles equations in his notebook with purpose and clear pissiness. What happened to him right before coming here?

"At least we agree on something." I gnaw on my pen. "Even though my problem is more the teacher than it is the book."

He scoffs. "'Tis a poor musician who blames his instrument."

"Excuse me?" I say even though I heard him.

"Nothing," he mumbles.

Daaamn . . . I shift around in my seat. Well, maybe he's right. Maybe it's not my teacher's fault. Maybe I'm just . . . plain . . . stupid. How nice of my peer tutor to point that out.

"Too bad you got me. Sabine is better at chemistry than I am. But I suppose for Rooney's class, I can help you well enough."

'Well enough'? How formal art thou, Gordon. All this, and he hasn't even formally introduced himself. Granted, it's understood that we probably know each other's names, but I still find it annoying, as if he assumes we probably won't be friends anyway.

"Great. So let's get started, Gordon Spoo . . . Spoo . . ."

"Spudinka." He looks straight at me underneath the hair hanging in his face. I never noticed before that his eyes are the exact color of swamp reptiles. "It's Russian."

"You're Russian?"

"I was born in Boston, but my grandparents came from St. Petersburg, so yes, I'm Russian. If you must know my family history."

"Uh, I was just being polite." I clear my throat. "And since we're going to work together, you should know my name is Chloé, *not* Motor Girl."

He stares at the page under his nose. I shudder at his sudden resemblance to Mr. Rooney. I never knew spiral-bound books could have such a profound effect on people. "Nice to meet you," he says flatly, looking at his watch (obsolete, sweetie, use your cell phone). He turns some equations toward me. "We've already lost a good ten minutes."

Chemical equations are the root of all evil. I try to make sense of what he's written, but all I see are hieroglyphics. "Fire away."

Suddenly Gordon perks up a bit, happy to be talking about things that make sense in his head. "It's really quite basic. All you do is balance the left with the right. It's like this. Watch . . ."

He proceeds to explain that balancing an equation is

nothing more than showing how the reactants become products, and shifting around the numbers is the way of conserving the equation's mass and charge. He goes on for thirty minutes, giving examples, then solving the equations himself, *showing* how it's done, not like Rooney's sink-or-swim technique.

During this time, I notice that the very tips of his brown eyelashes are blond. What this has to do with chemistry is anyone's guess.

"Make sense?" he asks, looking up. Fine, so maybe his eyes are not quite swampy upon further inspection. "If I give you ten more equations like these, can you do them on your own?"

"Correctly?"

Gordon blinks. "Yes, correctly."

"Lighten up, Gordon. It was just a joke."

He smirks, writes down ten more equations, and slides the paper over to me. Then he pulls out his own notebook, opens it to the last page, and starts jotting stuff down. Wait: Is that an actual *planner,* with tabs, charts, and sticky notes? *Holy shish kebab.* What is going on in Gordon Spudinka's life that requires such detailed organization?

"What are you writing?"

He speaks without looking at me. "I'll worry about me. You worry about you," he says, pulling out a highlighter and dousing a page in fluorescent green. "And boy, does she have a lot to worry about," he mumbles to himself.

Oh, *no.* He did *not* just take a condescending tone. I tap my pencil on my cheek. "Do you mind not talking about me like I'm not here?"

The sigh that comes next is so forced, so heavy, that I realize the awful truth—I am his volunteer work. He's here, teaching a certified moron about chemical conversions only because it will look good on his precious transcripts. No doubt he'd rather be home, riddling planetary cyborgs with bullets in his darkened room, while other globally connected computer geeks send him messages—each of them using one of their fifty internet pseudonyms.

Poor Gordon. He has every right to be rude to me.

I shift around in my seat, trying to suppress my own sarcastic thoughts, but my blood is starting to simmer. So I fire back. "Are you totally anal?"

He stops writing and turns a confused glare on me.

"Like, do you believe that every scrap of brain activity must be recorded on paper before it escapes you? You can't make decisions 'cause you're always afraid it'll be the wrong one. Am I right?" I've heard of people like this. So the legends are true.

Gordon's right eye twitches. Whatever comes next can't be good. "What I do outside of here is none of your business."

"I only asked because you sounded so concerned about me when you said I have a lot to worry about, and I wanted to show that I care about you too. It's just in my personality to reciprocate."

"And how many personalities do you have exactly?" He gives me a facetious smile. "Four, five?"

I give a fake gasp. I'm actually proud of him. Gordon is not only cute but competitive as well!

Before I can answer, he tries to put an end to our peer-tutoring fun. "Why don't you just finish the problems I gave you so I can get home to *more important things*?" he says.

I knew it. I imagine flicking a bent staple off the end of my pencil right at Gordon's forehead. Smack! Right in the middle. One more . . . smack!

"More important things?" I stare at him in disbelief, but he just scribbles and scribbles, ignoring me as if I'm too insignificant to have a conversation with. "Hey . . . does God ever consult you for advice? Don't get mad at me, I was just wondering." Oh, yes, he wants a battle, he'll get one.

Gordon looks up at me, and I totally think he's going to suggest that I get paired up with a different tutor, someone who I'd get along with better, when I see something—a little smile emerging on his lips. "Yes, on occasion, God and I hang out."

He can kid! He may be human yet.

"For the record, you started it." I smile, much to my own chagrin.

"For the record, Motor Girl, you know nothing about me. So don't assume anything."

Hmm, I can't say he's wrong, even though he's a dork for calling me "Motor Girl" again. I *don't* know him. And he doesn't know me, so *touché*. "Same goes for you. I may not be the best at chemistry, but otherwise, I have nothing to worry about. I know I don't have to explain this to you, but I am not the illiterate imbecile you probably think I am."

In fact, except for losing Seth, my life is just spiffy. Keeping safe from any more heartbreak is my main goal. *That, not chemistry, is my biggest worry, Gordon.* Although balancing $C_3H_8 + O_2 = CO_2 + H_2O$ is quickly climbing the ranks.

"Well, now that that's squared off, can we please finish?" he asks.

"Fine."

We say nothing else. I work on the equations, trying my best to remember what Gordon explained. I just don't know why we're forced to study things we're not meant for. I don't have any choice, though, or I'll be handing Lolita over to my dad by the end of the school year.

"Time's up," Gordon says, starting to pack up his things. I glance at my cell. Three twenty-five. We have five more minutes. I spin the notebook around for him to check my answers.

His eyes speed over them left to right. "You may be a very well-adjusted individual, one who doesn't need to explain herself to me ever . . ." He leans over and proceeds to correct half of my conversions, putting a tiny *2* under the last chlorine symbol. "But I'm sorry to tell you that you still need a tutor."

"Right." I check out the grime clinging to the auditorium chairs.

"And for your information," he says, zipping up his backpack, "I'm not anal. But if that's how you perceive me, who am I to argue?"

"Good. And for *your* information, I don't have multiple personalities." I'll give Gordon props for one thing: Kidding or not—the guy knows how to push my buttons.

That's a first.

I collect my things and pack them carefully for the wet

ride ahead. Maybe the rain has died down by now and I can take Lolita on a slow coast home. It would be so nice to let the memory of this first tutoring session drip behind me until my head is empty. I put on my jacket, tuck my helmet under my arm. Maybe it's time to call a truce with Gordon, too. I hold out my hand. "Look, I really do appreciate your help. Sorry if we got off on the wrong foot."

He stares at my hand for a second, then takes it and shakes evenly, with no more or less pressure than my hand in his. "You're welcome. I'm sorry too." He smiles full out now, and—whoa—Gordon Spudinka has Spu-dimples!

I play it cool, but I can't seem to tear my eyes away from the cuteness that has suddenly appeared out of granite and stone. "See you next Monday," I say, holding my breath.

"Monday," he repeats and takes off toward the stage.

I head out of the auditorium, letting the doors slam shut behind me. Wow. I don't know if I want to slug him or hug him. I have never had such a hard time getting someone to loosen up. Gordon's sense of humor seems to be made of Sheetrock, or maybe he was just having a bad day. But there's definitely something about the dude. Or maybe I'm just a big idiot for dimples. *Shake it off, Chloé.*

The deluge has stopped, but not without leaving behind lakes and rivers in the parking lot. As I walk toward Lolita, I notice something on her. One of those fabric-lined plastic tarps. I quicken my pace, examining the alien object that someone has had the nerve to lay on top of Lolita. Anybody who knows anybody who has a motorcycle knows they do not—and by *not* I mean NEVER—touch another person's bike, much less put anything on top of it.

I reach down to take off the rough cover. Up and over. Hundreds of water droplets converge and stream down, splattering my boots. I run my hands over Lolita's flames, feeling her paint job, which cost more than one month of Seth's rent and utilities put together. Still smooth. No nicks, no scratches. *Nada.* Not only is she fine, she's perfectly, happily dry.

Four

Obviously, the misguided soul who left the tarp was unaware of basic motorcycle ethics, so I can't bring myself to actually be mad, but Seth would have been. I can't take the tarp with me, so I fold it up as best as I can and drop it off behind the first column in Building B's hallway.

Who would even care enough to cover Lolita like this? Rock would, but he knows better. Besides, I've never seen this tarp in his trunk before. Gordon did come in wet from outside, but we're not exactly friends, more like I'm a tick on his after-school butt.

Oh, well. Whoever did it was just trying to be nice.

I ride by Rock's, hoping to steal him away so he can help

me with Lolita's leak today. His garage door is open, the Mustang's hood is up, but another car sits in the driveway, and it's not Amber's Xterra. *See?* This is exactly why I haven't set foot in his house in years, why we usually see each other at my house instead. I don't want anything to do with his player activities. I rev up Lolita, positive he can hear me. I don't care who is screaming in his bed, my pipes are louder.

I spend the next two hours driving around aimlessly, reveling in Lolita's pipes just like Seth used to. He always said that something mystical happens when you start a Harley. When I was little I didn't understand what he meant, but as soon as we put on Lolita's slip-fit mufflers, performance and sound were never the same again. Lolita's deep grumble would send vibrations throughout my legs. "Do it, Sethie, gun it!" I'd yell, clinging to his back, my hair flying around like an auburn-haired Medusa.

At my request, Seth would make Lolita go faster. I didn't know it then, but she asks for speed. Demands it. Seth would grip her ape hangers and squeeze until we were soaring. I wish I could tell you that riding with my uncle was like flying, transcending onto another plane, or becoming one with the Earth, but that would only be scratching the surface. It was so much more than that.

Mystical.

Unfathomable.

Fathomystic, maybe?

My mother would say "dangerous" and "reckless."

For being Seth's sister and hailing from a family of Harley riders, that is some serious blasphemy. She insists I will understand the dichotomy when I have carried children in my womb, given birth to them through tears of resignation and joy, and nourished them from my own body. Then, she says, I will start to see Lolita as death on wheels. Once, I told her that I *did* understand her "giving birth" scenario, because Seth and I ordered six-piston chrome bagger calipers for Lolita, then waited nine weeks for them to arrive, but she didn't think that was very funny.

The thing is—she should know better than anyone—once a biker, always a biker.

There comes a magical moment when you just *get* the connection that happens between human and machine, and that's when you become a biker for life. Lately, I've started to wonder if I got this affinity for motorcycles from just hanging out with Seth, or if my birth parents were the same way. I've always accepted that I'll never know, since my adoption case was closed, which means my birth parents and adoptive parents know nothing about one another. But I know there are ways to try and locate them. If I ever decide to, that is.

If only I could without hurting Mom and Papi.

Finally, the sun begins to descend behind the strawberry fields by my house. Lolita's tires cut through inches of this afternoon's rain, and the droplets fly up, striking my face like super-fine acupuncture. Gotta squeeze in at least one adrenaline rush before I get home. I up-shift to fifth and take the last stretch of straight road at sixty-five.

"Aaiieee!" My scream blends with the screaming of the engine.

Somewhere in my head, I hear my uncle's tenor-smooth voice laugh. *Atta girl, Chlo.*

❀ ❀ ❀

Our driveway is full of stuff that Papi's trying to sell as part of his New Year's resolution. But after three nights now, it's still around. His quest to empty our garage of my mother's junk while she is distracted with postnatal life is failing miserably. Pre-babies, she never would have allowed such a thing, but at the moment, she is nursing two three-month-olds and is too hormonal to even care. Besides, who would want a velvet portrait of the twelve signs of the zodiac, especially one with a coffee stain in the bottom left-hand corner? Salvation Army, Father, Salvation Army.

I ease Lolita in between a shrunken head torchière and a six-level shoe rack holding a library of bills older than I am. On a folding chair next to it, Papi sulks over the enormous task of feeding old bills one by one into his new paper shredder.

"How was the dock, *linda?*"

I pull off my helmet and scratch my head. "I wasn't at the dock. I'll go after dinner."

"You shouldn't be riding late every night."

"It's not that late, and it's not every night. At least you know where I am."

"Hmm," he says over the shredding noise. He knows I'm not a difficult child and that all I ever ask for is to ride. Overall, I am one cooperative kid. *"Mira esto."* He changes the subject. "It even shreds credit cards. Isn't that great?"

"Incredible." I bend over to kiss his cheek. His white Hanes T-shirt smells like gasoline, fish, and the open sea. I could smell him all day.

"How's Lolita running today? Did you and Rock tune her up yet?"

"Not yet. Next time he comes over, we'll get started."

"Tell him about the leak."

"He knows, Papi." The sad fact is I can't take care of her the way Seth did. Sure, I may have learned a thing or two from being around him all the time, but I need Rock supervising my tinkering to make sure I'm doing it right. I already tried fixing the leak twice, but it's still leaking. "Mom inside?"

He nods, but before I can take another step, he holds up his hand. "¿Las llaves?"

I drop the key into his palm so he can take his usual ride while waiting for dinner. "All yours."

I find my mother on the couch, babies sprawled asleep on her open-shirted chest. She and the twins have red hair, a trinity of flaming heads. I kiss all three of them. My mom opens her eyes and mumbles, "Chlo, honey, can you turn the rice off?"

"Can't you just put the twinsies down, Mom?" I can't bear to call them by their given names—Carl and Sagan. Ugh. Believe me, I can only feel grateful she didn't go with Castor and Pollux. "They're never going to learn to sleep in their perfectly tended, never-before-slept-in cribs."

"Please, Chlo."

I head into the kitchen and turn off the burner. "What's for dinner besides rice?"

"Fish, veggies . . . the usual."

"You seriously need to start cooking again."

My dad fishes for Eddy's, a local seafood market, so it's

snapper, kingfish, or dolphin almost every night (the fish, not Flipper). With so much omega-3 oil running through my veins, you'd think I'd be a Pisces, but alas, I'm a Sagittarius— ruled by Jupiter and Neptune. In other words, I have no ambition. I am a wanderer, an observer, not a scientist. At least that's what my astrology-obsessed mother has told me my whole life. The truth is, I am entirely more left-brained than she gives me credit for, and she might know this if she observed tangible evidence once in a while. Still, I'm not left-brained enough to understand chemistry.

My father, on the other hand, doesn't understand why I'm failing Rooney's class. He thinks I should have a passion for it, given my love of astronomy, as if all sciences were the same. At least he's on the right track, although he can be delusional too, at times. After all, he *is* outside waiting for strangers to buy Mom's junk.

"Is Rock coming for dinner?"

"Not sure, Mom. He might be busy tonight." I don't mention what or who he seems to be busy with over at his house.

"Hmm. I keep saving food for him, but then your dad ends up eating it the next day."

"Maybe it's better if you don't save him anything," I suggest with a shrug. "I'm sure he'll find food somewhere. You know Rock." If I were to tell her exactly what he's up to, she'd never believe me. *Sweet little Rock, a womanizer? Surely, you must be imagining things, Chloé.*

"How was tutoring?" Mom asks, trying to adjust the bandanna holding her hair back without waking the babies. The twinsy in blue stirs a bit. *Carl, green. Sagan, blue.*

I take Baby Sagan from her so she can rest an arm. He settles against my chest without a hitch. I love his little red eyebrows. "Good. I think it's going to work," I lie. "Hi, baby . . ."

"Did you get Sabine?"

I grab some silverware with my free hand and finish setting the table for her. "I did at first, but they switched me to this guy named Gordon. Isn't that an oldish name?"

"It's a perfectly nice name. And? How is he?"

"He explains better than Rooney does." I grab some of the used plastic cups scattered about that my mother insists we use to save water and time and toss them in the trash when she's not looking, then I add, "But he's full of himself."

"Aries?" my mother asks, like I should've gotten all his pertinent zodiac information in our first session.

"I don't know. I'm not going to ask him."

"Or might be a Scorpio. Find out next time, would you, honey?"

"*Arrgh.* The insanity!" I head for the babies' room, which is decorated to look like a purple sky with twinkling stars.

"What are you *arrghing* about?" Her voice carries down the hall. I've almost got Baby Sagan nestled in his bed where he should be, between two rolled-up blankets, when he wiggles in protest, then finally lets out a piercing wail. I pick the little sucker back up and carry him all the way back to my mother's boobs.

"Colette's coming, so can you make sure we have some seltzer?" she says above the surround-sound crying. Marraine's name always sounds pretty when it rolls off my mother's tongue.

"Uh, I was supposed to tell you that, sorry." I check the A/C closet, where we keep extra two-liter bottles of soda, hoping to get dinner over with as quickly as possible so I can once again hit the road.

Surprisingly, Rock does make it to our house in time for dinner, and my mom puts out an extra plate for him. "Thanks, Vero. You're the freakin' best," he tells my mom. I know he appreciates my family, especially since his dad works late every night, then leaves early every morning, leaving Rock to his own defenses, but does he have to say "freakin'" to my mom?

"Not a problem," she tells him with a smile. "Just get your disgusting shoes off my chair." Which he does with a sheepish grin.

"Nerd," I mumble. My dad grins at us from his seat, and we all settle down to eat.

Once we're done, Rock begins furiously texting Amber from his phone (at least I think it's Amber) while I listen to the adults in my life as they laugh and tell stories. Mom and Marraine's voices blend together to finish each other's sentences. Mom is six years older than Marraine, but they've been best friends since Marraine was fourteen. I always thought that was cool of my mom to be friends with a girl so much younger. It just goes to show that connections between people happen, regardless of age.

Papi and Mom were both twenty-one when they got married. They adopted me right away, agreeing to leave childbirth until later. But it happened much later than they expected—sixteen years to be exact. Now I have beautiful little brothers, but is it wrong of me to feel a bit jealous that our mom is *their* flesh and blood but not mine? I try not to think about it that way, but the thought persists. Other thoughts insist on persisting too. In fact, ever since Seth died this summer . . . it's like a dust cloud of persistent thoughts has kicked up in my life.

Like, what if Papi is the next to go? Or my mom? What do I do in the unlikely event that they *all* die in the same plane crash while I stay behind in small-town Florida City with nobody but Rock and some alligators? Then what? Then I'll have no family left. And no family left not only means no one to love, but no one to ask questions to. Then I'd never know if my birth parents loved the stars like me, or made up weird words like me. Because Mom and Papi wouldn't be around to tell me the name of the adoption agency they used. So, it's stuff like this I would love to talk to Mom about, but I don't want her thinking I don't love her enough. So I'm really trying to ignore all this as best as I can. They are the most awesome parents anyone could ever hope for, and I should focus on that.

After dinner, Rock and I wash the dishes. Or rather, he leaves half the plates all sticky and I fix them when he's not looking. Then he kisses each of us on the cheek, shakes my dad's hand, and is off again. "Later, Chlo."

"Don't you want to come to the dock with me?" I ask. We used to hang out there every day. Now he's always running off somewhere. "You wanted to talk to me, remember?"

"I know. But something came up. I'll call you later."

"Fine," I say, hearing him leave through the front door. "Someone lock up after me!" he calls.

I finish the dishes by myself and watch my parents shuffle around the kitchen putting things away. Papi's hand on Mom's lower back reminds me that they are lotto lucky. Still together, still making babies, still very much in love after seventeen years of marriage. I hope to find that kind of love one day. Until then, I do my best to help them, taking a baby into my arms to give my mother a break so she can make me an after-dinner espresso, for example. But as much as I love being with them—I really mean it, they are *ultra-fabacious*, a word that suits them *ultra-fabaciously*—I can't wait for dinner to be over.

The winter night sky awaits.

Five

The Murphys were a family I knew in elementary school who lived a few miles away. I used to hang out at their house and play with Irene Murphy, who was my age. She and her family were brutally murdered. All of them. And their ghosts still haunt the banks of this estuary . . .

Kidding.

Actually, they moved to Montana, because Mr. Murphy felt that Florida City—a sleepy migrant town that owes its existence to strawberries and tomatoes—was getting too "busy." But I overheard him talking to his wife one time, and I think the real reason they left was that he was sick of all the "damned immigrants." Considering that Papi's parents were "damned immigrants," I always felt defensive about that comment.

It's been years since they left, but I still think of the Murphys and their seven kids every time I hang out on their dock. Their house—a true fixer-upper that never sold—fell into ruin, which worked out great for me, because their backyard is now my private retreat. In fact, this dock, overlooking a stretch of mangrove estuary, is where I first saw a cat have kittens. It's also where I first spotted the rings of Saturn with Irene's rusty telescope. That was, and still is, one of the most awesome days of my life.

I don't know why everyone prefers city living, where you can't see a single star or planet. About five years ago, when Rock and I paid his mother an unusual visit in Kendall, we climbed to the roof one night to watch the stars, but it was like they had all gone into hiding. Then, Johany, her boyfriend's son, found us and started calling all the airplanes on the way to Miami International Airport shooting stars. Rock and I rolled our eyes. A ten-year-old who thought a burning meteorite had blinking red and white lights on it had to be a Gifted Child Extraordinaire. Soon after that, Rock's mom and GCE's father got married, turning GCE into Rock's stepbrother and the biggest reason why Rock rarely sees his mother anymore.

Why I'm thinking these things instead of studying is beyond me. Many things are beyond me lately. Like why Seth had to go and get leukemia at thirty. Like why he had to slip into a coma before a bone-marrow transplant might have helped him. Or, like Gordon *Spudoinky*. What is *up* with that guy? He's annoying but at the same time very intriguing. I liked the way it seemed we were about to kill each other, but then he just grinned big, amused at how far we had let the whole thing escalate. It *was* sort of funny. And that smile made me forgive everything. Weird.

I close my eyes and listen to the swamp. The usual frogs and crickets fight for air time. There's also the occasional sound of something surfacing in the water—a fish or snake or maybe even an American crocodile. None of them mind that I'm here because I'm not posing a threat. I'm just one of them—at home, in my little slice of heaven. I don't bother them, they don't bother me.

I lie on my back and stretch across the wooden planks. A shooting star—a real one—streaks from the east all the way across the sky. That was big. I used to wish on them a long time ago. It stinks how you learn the scientific explanation behind something magical, and then it stops being extraordinary. But for old time's sake . . .

I wish life could stay this simple forever.

I know it's a naïve thing to wish for, but as evidenced by the way I almost couldn't handle visiting Rock's mom in Kendall, the idea of going off to college, and of course, Seth's death, I'm just not good with change.

Six

The next Monday a cool front moves in, making every cat and dog in the neighborhood act frisky and every human wear sweaters more appropriate for skiing than fifty-five-degree weather. After a week of Rock's being missing in action I doubt I'll see him this morning, but as I open the front door, sure as shit, there he is. Asleep on my porch swing, arms folded over his chest, chocolate-chip granola bar at his head, courtesy of Mom.

"Don't you have a bed?" I ask, stepping out and closing the door behind me.

He mumbles something, like *nrwr.*

I reach down and hold my cold orange juice against his forehead. He stirs around. "Where have you been for a whole week?" I lock the door and walk over to the open garage. "Never showed up to talk last week. Never answered my calls. Amber trouble again?"

"Something like that," he mutters in a way I've come to recognize as "there's more, but you wouldn't care." Rock used to tell me everything, but lately, I think he's getting my vibe that I'm tired of hearing about it. "I'll tell you later. Right now, we're late."

"Right. Because you care so much about getting to school on time. Way to avoid the subject." I finish the juice, place the cup next to three other old cups on a shelf in the garage, then back Lolita out into the street. I close the garage door and start the engine.

Chewing his granola bar, Rock gets up, walks over to his car and gets in. With his door open, I can see jeans, shirts, underwear, and socks thrown in the passenger seat. He's been sleeping somewhere else. *Don't ask, don't tell.*

As we leave my street, he flashes his high beams—the signal that he's giving me a head start. *Ha!* I don't need one, but I'll play his game. As soon as we're on the Turnpike, I blast Lolita to eighty miles an hour, giving Rock a run for his money. When I look in my side mirror, I see he's gaining, so I speed up. Soon, he's neck and neck with me, thinking he's going to pass. How very optimistic and Libra of him. I slow down slightly to give him false hope.

When I look into the Mustang, he glances over and blows me a kiss. As if that will distract me. I lower my body so that my head is even with the handlebars, as aerodynamic as I can get on a cruiser, and wait for the right moment. Then I blast it. The car ahead of me moves into the left lane just as I do, so Rock has no choice but to swerve in behind me, following me past a line of traffic and onto the exit ramp, or else he's off to the Keys.

I check my mirror, eager to see him banging his steering wheel in frustration, the way he sometimes does. This time, his green eyes disappear into a bright, content smile. Did he just let me win?

I kick the clutch harder than is reasonably necessary.

A part of me keeps wishing I would bump into Gordon in the halls again, like I did last week, but Brain Boy and I run in different circles. I'll admit I'm looking forward to peer tutoring this afternoon, curious to see how we'll bounce off each other this time. From the way things ended last time, I already saw that he's not always uptight, that he can smile as well as return a sarcastic serve. I think my mother might be off in assuming he's a Scorpio. Gordon has a nice streak in him. More like a Leo.

Seven classes and two naps later, I stumble into the auditorium. Almost everyone is already studying with someone. But Gordon sits alone. I look at my cell. I'm only two minutes late. Excellent timing!

I plop my helmet down in the ass-bucket next to him. "What's your sign?"

He looks up, brushing his bangs aside with his pencil. "Excuse me?"

"My mother needs to know."

Gordon squints in confusion. I must remember not to joke with him or else he loses track of everything. "Tell your mother I'm sure she's a great woman, but I'm too young for her."

Ha!

"She's an astrologist, and I thought you weren't into funny."

"I thought you *were* into changing your clothes." He's looking at my black Hog's Breath baby T, getting a validated stare at my chest. *So I wore the same thing last Monday, big whoop.*

"It's not the same shirt."

"It looks like the same one."

"Might you have anything constructive to say to me today?"

"Change your clothes?"

"I just told you . . ." I start to say, but then I see he's suppressing a cute, dimply smile. Aha! So that's his game—getting my blood to start boiling, then playing *gotcha*! "You're bipolar, you know that?"

He chuckles. "Obviously, you don't know what *bipolar* means, to be using the word so loosely. Having bipolar disorder is more than just mood swings."

I roll my eyes. Before he launches into a hefty discussion straight from the annals of psychiatric medicine, I pull out my notebook and pen. "Don't get smart with me, Brain Boy." I glance up and notice that Sabine's peer, Francine, isn't here yet, so she seems to be casually attempting to overhear our conversation while she arranges her notebook, pen, and paper clips in front of her. *What* is her deal?

"Why are you all chipper today anyway?" I ask, focusing back on him.

He pauses, probably trying to decide how much he

wants to share with me. "I was invited to attend a preview orientation at MIT."

"MIT?" Impressive.

"It's a university," he explains.

"I know what MIT is! I'm not a bonehead, for crissake, Gordon!"

"Sorry."

"But you're not even a senior yet."

"That would be why I'm excited."

"Oh."

Apparently, the point of peer tutoring is to make your peer feel as stupid as possible. In which case, Gordon is doing a *stupendicular* job. *Stellacular* even. "Well, congratulations then."

"You sound so thrilled for me."

"No, I am. That's fantastic, Brain Boy."

He tilts his head at me, a genuine moment of interest in something I have to say. "Why do you call me Brain Boy anyway?"

"It was either that, or Mensa Man."

"Hmph." He looks at his watch then turns some equations to me. He's thrown in some new elements and extra symbols this time. "I'm not a member of Mensa. But my brother is."

Whoa. Where was I when God handed out intelligence genes?

"He's at Harvard." Scribble, scribble. "Medical school."

"Wow. How threatening that must be for you." I did not mean that as cruelly as it sounded.

But Gordon doesn't even blink twice. "You're not kidding. Try following in the footsteps of a brother who found a genetic risk factor for African Americans with prostate cancer."

"Ouch."

"Exactly."

I hit the nail on the head. He's entirely obsessed with his brother's success. But I guess if my older sibling paved a path of academic impossibility, I'd have an overly detailed organizer and weird sense of humor too. Come to think of it, it's kind of nice seeing Gordon this way. Who knew he had vulnerabilities of his own?

Gordon's eyes focus on a particle of dust suspended in midair for a moment before settling back on the notebook. Honestly, I don't know why he's excited about this orientation. Doesn't he want a life beyond professors, libraries, and highlighters? And academic clubs? Lots and lots of honor societies? He'll never know what it is to sit at the Murphys' dock and contemplate dark-energy theories and the vast immensity of the universe.

I think about his goal-oriented lifestyle and a wave of *melancholiosity* comes over me. Poor Gordon. It must suck to rush through the best years of your life, hurrying to graduate, hurrying to get a job, hurrying to join the workforce, all before you're even old enough to legally drink. This is serious. Gordon needs an intervention.

"What do you do on weekends?" I ask, even though he is now so absorbed in an orientation packet pulled from his backpack that he probably didn't even hear me.

He looks up at me. "What do you mean?"

"What. Do. You. Do. On. Weekends." I stare at him. "Do you surf? Do you read? Do you bake rugelach? Do you—"

"I get it." He cuts me off, eyelids at half-mast.

"It was a simple question."

"There is no such thing," he says, all serious, and I can't help but notice that his boyish face makes my stomach crunch up. So do his smooth hands. I wonder if Sabine felt the same way when they were together. *Were*, a word I try to send her telepathically, but she doesn't look up from her seat, so she must not have heard me.

"Yes, there is," I say, shaking off the thought. "And? What's the answer? You must do something with your time. Even doing nothing is doing something."

He waves his pencil around, hesitating. "I . . . I play computer games. I read. Actually, I . . . play more games than I read . . . whatever. Why are you asking?"

Hold up. Yeah, why *am* I asking? Why do I care about Gordon *Spadanky* anyway?

"Look," I say, waiting for voices of reason to pop into my head and tell me how dimples and cuteness should not override cockiness when it comes to liking certain boys. Nope. No voices today. I play with my pencil. "Why don't you take a break from your tests, college prep, and all that for a while? I know an awesome place where you can relax and not think about anything. You'll love it, I swear. There's a whole world out there."

The words are out of my mouth before I realize that I've never invited anyone to the Murphys' dock before besides Rock. It's my private sanctuary . . . yet I've just invited Gordon there. What is wrong with me?

"There's a whole world out there," he repeats slowly. "Did a fortune cookie tell you that? Or a cartoon princess?"

I throw up my hands. Why do I bother? "Forget I said

anything. From now on, we will only speak about atomic mass and nuclei."

"Sorry." He taps his pencil on the desk. "It's just . . . why do you assume I've been missing things?"

I face him. "Because you said you play games all weekend, and well . . . I'm sorry, but there's more to life than that."

He ponders this. "Maybe for you. Not for me."

I should've expected that answer. I shrug. "Whatever. I was just trying to be nice."

We're quiet for a minute and I think the subject is closed, but then, "You realize it's counterintuitive, right? How I'm supposed to let a girl who rides a motorcycle to school and is failing chemistry teach me about the things I've been missing?"

"Gordon," I say, raising my eyebrows, "you said you weren't going to judge me."

"I never said that."

"Yeah, you did. Last week. You said I shouldn't judge you any more than you should me, blah, blah, blah."

"No, I didn't."

"Would you—" I grunt. Does he have to go and challenge everything? "Just call me this week and we'll hang out." I write my number down on the corner of the notebook page, rip it off, and hand it to him. "If you want. If not, it's fine. I don't care."

He sits there looking at the scrap of paper in my hand. "You don't have to give me something in return for helping you, you know," he says, smirking. "I do this for free."

"*Pfft.* I know why you do it. Your transcripts. And we both know that nothing in life is free."

"Was that from the same fortune cookie or a different one?"

I glare at him. Nice. You try to be friendly with someone and they mock you. "You're impossible."

"I was kidding." He smiles.

I smirk back.

"Maybe I'll call. But I'm just letting you know now, you don't want to do this."

"Do what?"

"Get involved with me. I'm not the type to just hang around. And I have three tests on Monday to study for." He sighs so big, you'd think I was asking him to give up his life for all eternity.

"Well, I hope you'll take me up on it, but if not, it's cool." Then I focus my energy back to the strange world of electrons and neutrons. How anybody ever studied stuff smaller than dust is just batty.

Ms. Rath announces the end of today's session, tells us to have a pleasant week and to study hard. She doesn't say what to study though, so I'm in accordance no matter what.

Gordon and I look at each other and grin, packing away all our stuff. "So call me," I say, "if you get tired and want a change of scenery."

He nods, even though he still looks unsure. "If it means you'll leave me alone." He laughs.

"Oh, and . . ." I think about the best way to ask him this without sounding cheesy.

"Leo," he blurts. I was going to ask him about the tarp over my bike last week, but he's zipping up his mightily stuffed backpack with such a cute smile, that I can't bring myself to interrupt him. "Tell your mom I'm a Leo."

Seven

It's Friday afternoon, and I've decided to try to fix Lolita's leak again on my own. Or at least stare at her with tools all around me. Rock's not answering his calls—again—which means I will have to wait until he comes up for air from whatever evils he is up to.

I try to loosen a lug nut with a wrench, but it's on there pretty tight. Nope. This sucker is not coming off. It's times like these that remind me that boys are useful for something, even stupid boys who let me win during morning races instead of losing with integrity. The universe interprets my thoughts as a plea for help, and the familiar rumbling of an engine I'd recognize anywhere arrives in my driveway. A car door opens then shuts.

"Don't think I need your help tuning her up, because I most certainly do not," I call out.

Rock walks up and towers over me. "Well, I didn't know you needed my help, so that couldn't be why I came."

"Good, because I was kidding. I do need you. Grab a wrench."

"Aw, shit. I knew I'd get trapped here. What is it about your house?" He sits on the ground next to me and surveys the damage.

"It's a black hole of love. You can't help getting sucked in. Your charms are powerless here."

"You're right about that." He takes the wrench from my hand and proceeds to use arm strength to loosen the bolts—arm strength that my XX chromosomes did not give me at conception. In thirty seconds, he has managed to take off five parts.

I watch him. He reminds me of Seth sometimes, the way he really gets into working on cars and bikes. My uncle may not have had too many marketable skills, but tinkering with Lolita was a true talent I will never have without someone here to help me. "There's leftover dolphin in the fridge for you, by the way." I speak over his shoulder. "My mom told me to make sure you ate it."

"Your mom rocks."

I smile. Any mom would be a great mom next to the one he has. But he's right, both my mom and dad are good to him. They let him sleep on our porch, eat their food, even trespass when no one's home. Rock pretty much has an all-access pass here. Even if he hasn't used it much since school started back up last week.

"So, let me ask you something," I say. "What was that ridiculous thing you did the other day when we last raced?"

"Please identify which ridiculous thing you mean."

"Don't play stupid with me. You know what I'm talking about. You let me win."

"No, I didn't."

"Uh . . . yes, you did. And I don't need special treatment."

"I would never treat you specially."

I laugh. "Specially?"

He makes a laugh sound in his throat.

"You're not getting soft on me, are you?"

He raises the wrench. "I am never soft."

I shove his shoulder with my foot. "Yeah, that's your problem, I would say. But so you know . . . when we race, we race for real. Got it?"

His phone beeps, indicating a text message. He grabs it quickly and reads. "Shit. Amber." He proceeds to send a pissed-off, rapid-fire reply, then throws his already damaged phone back down on the driveway.

"What's wrong?" I ask.

"Nothing. I gotta go. Call you later." He stands up to leave.

"Rock, you can't leave Lolita like this. I can't tighten her back up like you can."

"I'll come back tonight."

"Tonight will be too late."

"I promise," he says, jumping in his car, starting the ignition, and taking off before I can conjure up curse words strong enough to affect him. I hurl the wrench into the grass. Seth would've given me a hard look for treating tools with disrespect, so I quickly go and pick the damned thing back up. Then I head back to my damned bike and put her more or less back in the same damned condition she was in before I started.

At night, I'm at the Murphys' dock, flat on my back, watching the nightly show. When I was little, Seth used to point out Sirius to me because it was always the brightest star in the sky. It's weird to think that Seth is gone, while Sirius is still around and probably will be for another million years. Sometimes I wonder if he's near it right now, riding Harleys ever after through the galaxy.

Maybe I should get home. It's 10:34 P.M., and even the frogs have fallen asleep.

The weekend is here, and Gordon hasn't called yet. Probably won't, either. I accidentally-on-purpose ran into him twice this week, and both times, he smiled and said, "Motor Girl," and I said, "Brain Boy." It was really cute. I acted all casual, too, even though I screamed inside my head both times. I guess I'll have to accept that I have a bit of a Stockholm syndrome on my torturer—tutor, I mean. But it'll pass. Crushes always do.

My thoughts are interrupted by the Mustang's rumbling engine again. It stops twenty feet away and cuts, restoring the peace. Shoes crunch over gravel, and a heavy door closes. My personal bubble is about to be invaded, but it's a welcome invasion. "I was just about to leave." I let my words get carried out to space by a cool breeze.

A low laugh answers me. "How do you know it's me and

not some crazy freak here to murder you?" His edgy tenor voice makes me smile in spite of myself.

"Your engine, duh."

"Oh, 'duh', is it? You know, you really need to stop coming here alone."

"Can you give the chivalry crap a rest?"

"Sorry. Sometimes I forget you're a guy in a girl's body, that's all." His voice grows closer and is soon accompanied by a swaying beam of light.

"That's sexist. Speaking of which, flashlights are for sissies," I tell him.

He finally arrives at my head, the toe of his sneaker touching my hair, and shines the Maglite right into my face. "Only one way to find out if that's true," he says, dropping his voice a notch, his legs wide apart in a studly stance.

I squint. "Spare me. Turn that stupid thing off, you're messing up my night vision."

"Ooh, night vision," he says, planting his butt next to me, the familiar scent of Rock infiltrating my space. Coconut SPF lotion and musky skin. Not a bad combo, I assure you. "For you, my queen." He hands me a Styrofoam takeout container. "Sorry for running off on you earlier."

My queen? I raise an eyebrow at him.

"Why are you looking at me like that?"

"Because you've been acting weird."

"And that alarms you because . . ."

"True. You're always weird," I say, but I'm recognizing the familiar Rock pattern, the one where he starts latching on to me whenever things go sour with Amber, so I change the subject. "What is this?" I pop open the container, revealing a glorious slice of caramel flan.

He hands me a plastic spoon. "A gift from Ricardo's."

"Thanks." I dig right in and start devouring my present. "So what are we looking at tonight?"

"Nrff."

"Same thing we look at every night?" he answers for me. "Why do you look so damn far up for things, Chloé? When everything you need is down here?" He lies on his back, turns toward me, then stares at me for a while.

I hold the spoon with my mouth and slap his *stupendicular* arm. Crikey! "Shtop that." I glide the spoon through another velvety slice of heaven. "So what happened to you?"

He leans back on his elbows, and if it weren't for that whole friend thing, I would so lay my hand on his arm. "I went to see Amber."

"Ugh."

"I know, but I'm pretty sure it's over this time."

"Again?"

"I think she's seeing someone else."

"An exorcist, probably."

"Chloé . . ." he warns. "Be nice. I think it might be King Doof."

"What?" I squint, holding up my spoon. "Vince wouldn't do that to you."

"Doesn't matter." He pauses. His chest rises and falls slowly. "He can have her."

I roll my eyes. "You say that, but then you waste your time on her over and over. You're together. You're not together. You're together . . . which is it? Because it was *not*

Amber's car parked in your driveway last week."

He shrugs. "Yes, we're on and off. Okay. But it doesn't bother me, Chloé. I can take her or leave her. I don't love her like that. I just hate seeing her with anyone else. I can't explain it. It's a territorial thing. And as for the other car . . . which one do you mean?"

"Whatever," I say, rolling my eyes. "I can't keep up with your throngs of women, Rock, and I don't want to hear about them anymore. None of them. *Nadie. Nyet.* It's getting icky. Is this what you needed to talk to me about?"

"Not really." Rock can usually cover up anything with the flash of his smile, but tonight, he seems to waver. He says nothing else, closes his eyes.

I think I know where this is leading. So I redirect the conversation. "Hey, I've been meaning to ask. Did you put a tarp on Lolita last week?"

He lifts his butt to take his phone from his back pocket. "Why would I do that?"

"Someone covered her so she wouldn't get rained on. Someone trying to be nice, I guess."

"Who would be nice to you?" He lies down flat, smiling in the dark.

"Exactly." I bump his head with mine and try to imagine we are brother and sister, linked by astral cords. I've always wanted a close sibling, someone who would have a connection with me from birth, even if we were on opposite sides of the planet. What if I have one somewhere out there? Closer to me in age, that is. All the more reason to investigate my adoption case. I hope Baby Carl and Baby Sagan grow up to realize how lucky they are.

"Chloé, I have a question." He rolls toward me and props up his head. The way he says my name makes my stomach clench. This brother-sister fantasy was—*poof*—over before it ever began.

"Yeeees?"

"The thing is . . ." His face moves in on mine, and suddenly I can totally relate to all the girls who fawn over him. His soft breathing warms my cheek. The hairs on my arm stand straight up. Good thing it's too dark for him to see it.

"Rock," I interrupt him before he throws himself to the wolves. As hot as he may be, I won't play his game. "Amber dumped you. Now you're seeking me out. It's a pattern. Recognize it."

"Recognize what?"

"That you always do this. Fall hard for girls who don't care about you, then come crying when they drop you, acting like you want to be with me."

He wipes caramel from my mouth with a finger and sucks it off. I do my best to ignore this gesture. "Maybe that's because my experience with other girls reminds me that, in the end, *you* are the best."

I push him back away. "Don't complicate things."

"I'm not complicating anything. It's the truth." His eyes are killing me. They've always held power over me, but this is ridiculous. Then he goes and says this: "I'm going to die alone unless you save me, Chloé."

I look at him like the idiot he sometimes is. "Would you stop? You don't need to be saved. You just need sense knocked into you."

"Yes, and you're the only one who can do that." He traces my face with his finger. I hold my breath and try not to notice, but it's like trying not to notice that a Greek god has landed in your bathtub.

"No, I'm not."

"Fine. You're the only one I'll *let* do that."

"That's different." I turn my face away from him and up to the skies, hoping he'll do the same. "Isn't this a beautiful night?"

"Chlo, you're killing things."

"What *things*, Rock?" I face him again, dead serious this time. "There aren't any *things*. *Things* do not happen between us." I know he loves me, and believe me, I love him too. But if we ever became boyfriend and girlfriend, it would never be the same again, and I don't want to take that risk.

"Fine. *Things* do not happen between us," he says in a mocking tone. We lie there, watching the sky for what seems a long time. "How about if you kiss me then?" he asks. "That's all I want. One kiss." His eyelashes lower slowly. How could anyone say no to him? He leans in with those gorgeous lips, and all I have to do is touch them with mine to send him home happy. It's just hard to do when you don't know where else those lips have been today.

I've only kissed Rock twice before. Once when I was fifteen and I fell for his stupid "you are an amazing, amazing girl, you know that?" Then again last fall, when he brought a bottle of Parrot Bay out here and we actually tried counting all the stars, stopping around 284. That night I thought for a nanosecond that he was the best thing that had ever happened to me. But I had been coping with Seth's death and clearly wasn't thinking straight. Especially when it hit me: *This is Rock I'm kissing.* And hadn't he just told me about the twenty-year-old Pilates instructor he'd been with a few hours earlier? I remember sobering up real quick.

Before I can overanalyze the moment any longer, his lips touch mine—soft, warm, perfect. I wish I could say it's terrible, that there's nothing between us whatsoever, but I can't. Rock kisses *sooo* nice. I had forgotten. He is entirely more sensitive than girls give him credit for. Some people have said that we're a perfect match because of his love of cars and my love of riding, but I just don't see it. I have way more things I want to discuss with a boyfriend besides carburetors and firing time.

I think of Gordon and our charged conversations. I want something like that, but without all the hostility. And highlighters. And righteous attitudes. Forget it. I obviously can't think with this beautiful man kissing me.

Rock pulls back, and his eyes search my face. "You're not into this. You don't think I'm the one for you, do you?"

I take a good look at him. I see a wonderful guy, misguided though he may be—one who's always been there for me. But I've lost count of how many girls—women—he's been with. And I just cannot be with a player like him.

"I never said that." I turn my eyes back to Arcturus and the Milky Way, now becoming visible after settling on the horizon all winter long. "I just don't think it's that simple. Real love—soul mates—are very rare. Some people meet theirs when they're already old, and some people aren't lucky enough to meet theirs at all."

We're quiet for a minute while he thinks about this.

Maybe he's amused that I could be so skeptical. Or maybe I've shocked him into seeing the inevitable truth—that Rock is my best friend—no more, no less.

"Chloé Rodriguez." He sighs softly, closing his eyes. "You are one cynical little girl with your 'don't think' and your theories."

Somewhere in the darkness, a frog agrees with him. "Yeah? Well, at least I won't be going around my whole life living in total disillusionment, wondering why I haven't met my soul mate yet. At least I'll be realistically happy, not searching for anything out of this world."

His soft laugh vibrates next to me—a sad, sympathetic laugh. He can laugh all he wants, but on some deeper level, he knows I'm right.

Rock rolls onto his back and stretches his arms behind his head. He shuts his eyes against the flickering of a billion suns, as if Earth holds all the secrets he'll ever need. "With the way you come out here every night, baby doll," he says, sighing, "you could've fooled me."

Eight

Over the weekend, it rains nonstop. Again. This would be a great time to try to finish working on Lolita's leak in the garage, but once again, Rock's not answering my texts or calls. What is up with that boy? I sulk in my room, watching reruns of old shows and thinking about Friday night at the Murphys' dock. I can't believe he's ignoring me. Like he's such a relationships expert! Maybe he finally realized it takes more than sex to have a connection with someone and can't stand that it won't be me.

He should've quit while he was ahead, brought me the flan, and just talked about pistons. But *noo*, he just had to ruin it. Bad Rock. Bad, bad Rock. Ah, but that kiss! How could I call that ruining it? *Shake it off, Chloé.*

And what about Gordon? He'd better have a good reason for not calling, after I invited him somewhere on a *weekend*. That's what I get for giving two hoots about him.

I decide to forget about men altogether by logging a few hours at my computer. After the usual site hangouts, I stare at the empty search box and try to think of something besides sky patterns to research. Before I even know what I'm doing, I slowly type *adoption agencies Florida*, and my heart starts to beat a little faster. So many choices appear, but I can't seem to click on any of them.

Why do I care? What do I expect to find?

Well, for one, what if I have a brother or sister? Someone besides the babies, even though I love them, but God forgive me for saying this—someone who is blood related. Wouldn't I want to know that?

The rain hits my window almost horizontally, as if someone were sloshing it with big buckets of water. I'm mesmerized by the fluid swirls it creates as it glides down the glass.

What if I end up with an illness like Seth years from now? What if I need a blood transfusion from someone whose DNA is similar to mine? Aren't these good-enough reasons to search for my birth parents, or am I just rationalizing the simple fact that I want to know because I simply want to know?

My brain hurts. And the guilt I feel for thinking that I'm betraying Mom and Papi hits me so hard, I totally erase the search from my browser history, turn off the computer, and go see if any laundry needs doing.

❖ ❖ ❖

Monday morning.

Rock is not asleep on my front porch. He is not there at all, and we're already late for school. Is he mad? Because he has no right to be. I didn't do anything to him. *Did I?* I guess today's street ballet will be a solo act. Again.

At school, I pull out Lolita's kickstand and feel her weight as I lean her over. Scattered thunderstorms are predicted again for later this afternoon. Maybe that tarp wasn't such a bad idea. Up ahead, Vincent strolls onto campus, cigarette over his left ear as usual. He reaches the covered walkway when a girl jumps out from behind a column and attacks him with a huge kiss on the lips. I walk faster, trying to beat the bell, but then I notice who the girl is and slow down.

Blond hair, black ends. Amber.

Shitsters. Rock was right.

Freakin' Vincent. King Doof.

I'm surprised and yet . . . I'm not. If anyone likes to sample the variety here at Everglades High, it's Amber. And Vince is probably just happy to have Amber paying him any attention. Still, why do I feel like going over there and yanking her hair? Why doesn't she just leave Rock *and* Vince alone?

Vincent sees me and waves. Now I have to act nice. "Hey, Chlo. Heard you're getting tutored by that Russian dude."

"Who told you that?" Not that getting tutored is a big deal to Vincent, but still, I didn't go around broadcasting it.

"His ex—what's her name, Sabine?" he asks Amber.

"Yeah. She was talking to her friend in the office when

I was getting a late pass," Amber says, as if I asked her. "Apparently, she thinks you guys have a little more than *chemistry* tutoring going on, if you know what I mean." She laughs like such a lecherous fool, I want to slap her.

"Why would she think that?" I ask, remembering the way Sabine had looked over at Gordon and me last week. It's not like I have FREE SEX stamped on my forehead. Geez, talk about hypersensitive.

"I don't know, but you could've asked *me* for tutoring, Chloé. I would've schooled you." Vince joins the lecher-speak, and now I want to slap them both.

"Ha, ha. Funny. I'll see you guys later." I try escaping before *awkwardity* immobilizes me.

But Vince goes on. "Listen, we're having a party Saturday night at Amber's place."

They're having a party together already? God, that's so cute! Not. I register the momentary look of worry on Amber's face. You know, maybe I should go to this party just to piss her off. "Really? What time?" I pretend to be totally interested.

Amber cuts Vincent off before he can do any more damage. "Anytime after nine. But if you can't make it, we'll totally understand."

"Oh, no," I say. "I'm pretty sure I can make it. I can bring friends, right?" Wouldn't she just love me and Rock at her party? I wait, eyebrows raised.

"Whoever, dude," Vincent answers on her behalf, ringing her shoulders with his arm. "Bring your tutor." He laughs out loud. I can't imagine Gordon would ever want to go to a party with me. He'd probably feel like he'd been teleported onto another planet.

I smile. I wonder how people do it. How Amber can move on to Vincent when he's one of our buddies and obviously knows about her and Rock's jagged past, and how Vince can go for it. I know it'd make *me* crazy, if the guy I was seeing had been with another girl not long before and that girl talked about it like it was nothing. "Thanks, guys. I'll see you later."

Vince gives me a peace sign. He seems happy, but I don't know. I wave at them and veer off toward first period. Should I call Rock and tell him what just happened? Would he even care, now that he thinks I'm his soul mate?

I decide to call anyway. He doesn't answer. As usual. "Call me," I say when his voice mail picks up. "I have things to say."

"Chlo-ou-éee?" I hear an impatient voice calling. *Crap.*

"*Oui, Madame Jordan?*" I reply, turning toward her classroom.

"Don't *Oui, Madame Jordan* me. Why are you late again?"

I reach her and stamp a kiss on her cheek. "Because mornings like today's are few and far between, so we must stop to smell the palm trees?" I say in French.

"*Don't sass me, little girl.*"

I take off running. "*Je t'aime, Marraine.*" Godmothers are godmothers for a reason. They can't get angry at you. It would be totally against Jesus's wishes.

"*Oui*, you'd better be raising that grade with *Monsieur* Rooney, insolent child." Then she's mumbling something in French again as she withdraws into her classroom.

I run up the stairs, hurrying now because luck can't possibly be on my side *every* day of my life, and I am not mentally disposed to reciting any gases today, much less the noble ones. I take the stairs two at a time, feeling the awesome burn in my quads, when all of a sudden . . . he's there.

Say hello, keep it cool . . .

I slow down. From the look of it, Gordon is wearing new sneaks today. "Mr. Spudanka! Are you delivering another package to Henley's class?" I smile sarcastically.

"Spu*dink*a," he corrects me, smiling the same way he did all last week in the hall. There's something about seeing a usually serious person smile. Their whole face lights up. My eyes are drawn to him, even though I will *so* be asking for it when I walk through Rooney's door.

"Right, that's what I meant." I also see he's achieving a "chic-geek" look today. Still nerdy but somehow more aware of himself. What is this *je ne sais quoi* quality? Is his hair tousled differently? Or is it simply that Gordon is quite handsome upon closer inspection, in a young Ryan Reynolds sort of way?

"Sorry I didn't call you this weekend." He gives me a sheepish grin.

"What . . . the . . . oh, you mean . . . Hey, don't worry about it. I actually had tons of stuff to do." And by tons of stuff, I mean napping.

"Yeah, me too. I got caught up studying for a calculus test."

I stand there half smirking, half smiling . . . *smirkling*. He stands there *smirkling* too. We *smirkle* quite a bit. "Well, I gotta . . ." I say, pointing to Rooney's door. "You know . . ."

"Yeah, reciting the elements, I know." He smiles, and the Spu-dimples return to render me unconscious. *Mon dieu!*

I watch him rush off down the stairs. Even though he is still *malevoly* for having completely disregarded my attempt at connection this weekend, I think what just happened might actually be considered a breakthrough.

"Helium. Neon. Argon . . ." I pause to glare at some of my classmates who are snickering beyond reasonable control. From this angle, they have taken on a different look, like a crowd at a public hanging. "Kryptonite . . ." I can't think of which element comes next. All I hear is louder laughter all around.

Mr. Rooney squints as though I have suddenly become a misty cloud before his very eyes. "Kryptonite," he says, adjusting his bifocals, "is not on the periodic chart of elements, last time I checked, Miss Rodriguez."

I smile nervously. "I meant krypton." For some weird reason, standing there, providing the class with school-time entertainment, I could only think of two things: one, that this painful moment would be emblazoned in my mind for all eternity; and two, that I was glad Gordon wasn't there to see it.

Nine

Rock finally comes out of hiding, gracing me with his presence right after lunch. It's a mystery to me how administration has not caught on to his network of girls who not only do most of his classwork for him but forge notes and call in as his mother as well. If only I had *people* like he does, I could afford to skip school half the year too.

He catches up to me and presses his lips against my cheek, as if Friday night's awkwardness never happened. Sometimes I wish I was a guy so I could just pretend important emotional exchanges between people never took place.

I stare straight ahead. "You didn't have to ignore my calls."

"I didn't ignore you. I was busy."

"I don't want to hear it." I block his words with my hand.

He laughs like a dirty old man. "Trust me, you don't."

And there you have it. "You're sick."

I act like his attitude doesn't bother me, but obviously it does. How am I supposed to believe anything he tells me when he goes right back to old behaviors like that? Doesn't he care that he might be picking up germy diseases from his extracurricular activities, or that he might get someone he barely knows pregnant?

"I meant everything I said the other night, by the way," he says, taking my backpack and carrying it for me. Girls huddle like groupies as Rock walks by. Pretty girls. Girls who, for all intents and purposes, could get any guy they wanted. But Rock ignores them, his eyes focused on me.

"I'm sure you did," I say, scanning the halls.

"But it's not enough, right?" He smiles, his lips just barely parted.

I shrug. I don't know what to think anymore.

Am I crazy to keep my best friend at bay like this? Maybe. But the idea of us together is more than a little terrifying. What if it didn't work? We could never hang the same way again. There would always be weirdness in the air. Or the worst case . . . we may go separate ways and never talk again.

No likey.

Speaking of weirdness, Amber suddenly comes careening down the hall and catapults herself like an Olympic long jumper right onto Vince's back. I watch Rock's face carefully. Anyone who knows him the way I do would see his soul imploding right inside his glass skin. Amber is such a bitch—she even looks back at him for a second to make sure he notices.

But he turns away right as she does and locks his eyes on mine. "I knew it."

"I tried calling to tell you, but as usual, you didn't pick up. Don't let it get to you." I lean forward to kiss him somewhere between the cheek and the lips and let it linger. *Take that, Amber.*

He laughs and puts his arms around me. And then I'm lifted inches off the ground in one of those crushing Rock-hugs. "And that is why you rock," he whispers into my ear. I have to punch him so he'll put me down.

"Later."

"Later."

Did you hear the one about the girl who rides a motorcycle to school, and everyone thinks she must be a lesbian because she not only refuses hot guys who fawn over her but also has no real girlfriends?

Me neither.

As I sit here nervously waiting for Gordon to arrive, Sabine seems immune to the lesbian rumors. She glances at me anxiously, and I have to use all my willpower not to say, *"What?"* every time she looks over. She bounces in her seat, checking and rechecking the auditorium door. I tap my pencil against the desk. *Tap-tap-tap. Tappity-tap.* I hope it's not raining. I hope Mystery Tarp Putter doesn't get any more clever ideas while I'm here either.

Ms. Rath settles everybody down, but Gordon is not here yet. To pass the time, I close my eyes. Sven appears in a halo of snow and ice. Not only is Sven my fantasy ski instructor, but he is a distant cousin of Julio, the dream lagoon tutor. Sven's sparkling blue eyes work well to eradicate all thoughts of dimpled, invitation-refusing, MIT-bound chemistry tutors from my mind. I lay my head down and imagine Sven carefully guiding my hands over the ski poles, gripping them firmly, demonstrating how he wants me to hold them. We communicate through body language and a series of soft cries. Sven is great because he doesn't get the least bit cold when he pulls off his parka and T-shirt. He is a Norwegian snow god. *Je t'adore, Sven.*

But then Gordon arrives, plopping into the seat next to me, dissolving any plot advancements my Norwegian daydream might have made. "Sorry I'm late," he says.

Au revoir, Sven, cheri. I lift my head and peer up at him through tired eyes. "This is a recurring theme with you, isn't it?"

Out comes the organizer, the pen, an extra pad of sticky notes. "Let's go, Chloé. I have to get home to study, and you have to pass chemistry."

"What's the rush? Why must you get home?" I ask, scanning over some new equations and bonus question he's handed me.

He moves around his sticky notes as if prioritizing them. Suddenly, after a few seconds, he looks at me and says this: "What are you, my girlfriend now?"

Ouchies.

My super-keen senses tell me he is upset. The friendly

Gordon of this morning—*gone*—just like that. He reminds me of an old Rolodex thing my mom is storing in the garage for the day we might need one, except with moods instead of contact cards: pissed, bored, friendly, pissed . . . and *I'm* the one with multiple personalities?

"Well, I *do* come to you with issues on a regular basis, and you *do* smile at me in the hallways, so technically, we *are* seeing each other."

He cracks a teensy, tense smile, but that's it.

"What happened?" I ask. "Last I saw you, you were in a good mood. Did *someone* get an A-minus on a test or something?"

I start on the problems while he just stares blankly down at his organizer without really looking at it. "You know, you can mock me all you want, Chloé, but you'll never fully grasp how important it is that I succeed in this life. For you, failing might be an option. But for me, it's not."

My mouth wants to drop open. I shoot little laser beams at his hair with my eyes. It does not catch fire. I am disappointed. What is his problem? Why does he treat me like he likes me one second, then like I'm his worst enemy the next? And worse, why am I finding that incredibly sexy?

"I understand that, Gordon, which is why I want you to relax, or else you're going to kill yourself worrying about your classes and your grades and everything. Or does this have nothing to do with school?" I wiggle my eyebrows to suggest girl problems—Sabine problems, to be more exact.

He sighs. "It's my SAT coming up. I have to do better than last time if I want to make a good impression. Or else my choice of worthwhile colleges is limited. Plus, MIT has an early-entrance exam, which, if I pass, means I can get in before the start of the fall semester. Forget it, I don't even know why I'm bothering to explain this to you."

I narrow my eyes at him. "You know, you keep doing that . . . that . . . *thing* . . . where you just assume I'm too stupid to understand what it means to succeed in life. But I do, okay? I just believe that there should also be some room for good things . . . fun things . . . because sometimes we die too early." I pause to collect myself. *Calm down, Chloé.* "Forget it, I don't know why I'm bothering to explain this to *you*," I mumble, making sure he knows I won't take that crap from him.

"Look, I'm just stressed, Chloé."

"Which is my point, Gordon. You have to wind down sometimes, or else you fall out of touch with yourself. I tried to help, however, *somebody* never called me."

"I'll wind down when I'm dead, and I already apologized to you about not calling."

"Augh," I scoff. "That is so Leo of you."

> Which of these substances will not conduct electricity
> well when in liquid form?

How the hell should *I* know? What do I care, and what makes Gordon the sort of person who can actually teach this to someone? I breathe deeply to release some of the tension in my shoulders.

We're quiet for twenty minutes, and strangely enough, it's not weird anymore. Gordon can snap at me, I can snap at him, but then we just settle into a comfort zone, and all is okay. I'm totally getting used to this relationship.

"Fine," he blurts into the silence between us, his head still down. He looks at his watch. "You win. Let's get out of here."

"Huh?"

"When I say go, pick up your stuff and head for the door."

"What do you mean?"

"Just do it. Ready?" He seems a little overanxious for someone about to walk out of class. It's not like he's going to rob a bank. Then again, this is Gordon. For him, it's a big deal. I feel my heart quickening at the spontaneity of his decision.

I wait for the signal. Whatever he has up his sleeve, I'm game. Besides, what can happen to us for leaving peer tutoring? It's voluntary!

"In three . . . two . . ." He pauses, glancing at Ms. Rath, who walks into the wings onstage. "One. Go."

I gather up my notebook, throw it into my backpack. A couple of kids in front of us turn around. "Emergency," I whisper, folding down the seat's writing desk.

They turn back around just as I'm headed up the aisle, through the EXIT doors, and into the hot sun. So much for those scattered showers. They must be scattered somewhere else. I smile, feeling my cheeks burn. Gordon rushes out behind me, arranging his backpack on his shoulder.

"What was that all about?" I ask. He looks like he just committed treason against Ms. Rath. "Are you okay? You look a little overwhelmed."

"Yeah." He chuckles. He has a nice bubbly laugh. He

should use it as often as possible. "I'm fine. I just needed to get out of there."

"Anything you want to share?" We stop in front of Lolita, and I slip on my riding jacket, start braiding my hair.

"I have two tests tomorrow—calculus and honors physics, and MIT's early-entrance exam is going to mean nothing if I don't get at least a fourteen hundred on my math SAT, so I have to study for that too. I'm not a genius, Chloé. I know you think I am. Everyone thinks that."

I nod. "Fine, maybe you're not a genius, but you're smarter than average, so don't try to hide it. Still, I get what you're saying about people making assumptions. People make them about me too."

He kicks the sidewalk. "So there you go. See, I have to work really hard to get the grades I get. Emile's never had to study for a damn thing, you know?" He mutters, lost in thought.

"Who?"

"Emile, my brother," he clarifies.

"Oh. This is why you made me follow you out here?" I realize it's a leading question, but I like torturing him.

Gordon thumbs the belt loop on his jeans. "I guess I owe you for trying to get me out of the house. I know what you're trying to do, and I appreciate it. Don't misunderstand me, it's just . . ." He pauses.

"It's just what?"

He squints at me, cocking his head slightly. Then he scans the entire parking lot, his answer getting lost somewhere out there. I don't know what's at the heart of his stress, but it doesn't take a real genius to know that Gordon wanted to be alone with me. I just want to hear it. "Where's this magical hangout place that you must take me to?"

I smile. Little does he realize what he's about to gain by going to the Murphys' dock. "Not far from here. Maybe ten, fifteen minutes. Why?"

"Do you always ask so many questions? I'll follow you."

"You sure?"

"Your window of opportunity is going to close if you don't start leading me there now." He smiles, walking away.

"All right, where are you parked?"

He points to an old tan BMW parked on the street near the office.

"Okay, I'll meet you out there, and you can follow me."

We're crossing the tutor-student line and heading into unknown territory. But I think that's okay, because Gordon fascinates me. I know he's overworked, way too serious, and even cocky at times, but still . . . I get the feeling there's this whole other side to him that I can't completely see yet. I may not know what it is, but it's there. And that alone is enough to pull me in.

Ten

Private sanctuaries are private for a reason—so one can reflect, loiter, and nap without mothers interrupting to ask that you hang up the laundry before it rots in the washing machine. But Gordon looked so defeated, so tortured standing there, I knew he desperately needed a break, and I don't know of a better place for one.

Given our petty arguments, I realize how inconsistent it is to be sharing my sanctuary with him, but inconsistency is consistent with the way Gordon makes me feel. I guess that's what people mean by love-hate relationships. Like now: I feel strangely hyper as Gordon follows me. *Wait, he is still following me, isn't he?*

I check the mirror. Yep. Still there.

I turn onto the Murphys' street, where the weeds grow longer than they should and the houses could use a new coat of paint. I gun Lolita down the road, thrilling at the dip, then turn into the Murphys' driveway.

Gordon follows, but I know that dip is just not the same in his car. I pull up to the gravel road leading to the dock and cut the engine. Gordon's tires crunch over the ground and come to a stop. As I take off my gear, I notice him sitting frozen in his car. That boy has issues. I nod to encourage him. A few feet away, an egret watches us.

Finally, Gordon gets out and trudges over. "Where are we?"

The buzz and chirping of a hundred or more insects in the sawgrass welcome me. "Do you mean literally or figuratively?"

"Any explanation will do."

I start down the path, Gordon at my side. "Literally, we're at an estuary. Figuratively, this is my home."

He nods with a smirk.

"I may as well live here. I'm always here." We step onto the old planks and walk up to the dock's edge. The water is slimy brown today. Between the patches, you can see pipefish feeding off the surface slime.

Gordon stands there, arms folded. "Is this the place you desperately wanted me to see?" He smiles, playfully bumping my arm with his side. Gordon is a big, strong boy, so I nearly fall over when he does this. *Not* something I'm used to.

I sit on the dock, dangling my legs over the edge, and lean back. "Make fun of it all you want, but stay here long enough and you'll see this place is magical."

"This place is in desperate need of environmental intervention, is what it is."

"The water's *supposed* to look this way," I say. "It's fresh and salt mixed together. There's a whole delicate biodiversity thing going on."

"I know. I was just teasing." He sits next to me, blocking the sun. We look out and listen to the sounds of the swamp, taking in nature's voices, but Gordon still seems uncomfortable. He's too quiet.

What would Rock do if he saw me here with Gordon? Probably ask a million questions. *Who's the dude? Why'd you bring him here? You think he's hot, don't you?* In my peripheral vision, I notice Gordon peering out at some movement in the water. I take the opportunity to check him out real quick. He hasn't shaved in a day or two. When he's off guard, it's easy to see that Gordon is pretty hot.

What makes him irresistible at the moment, though, is that he's here with me. He could be doing his thing at home, studying, playing Sudoku, filling out college applications, but he's not. He's making an effort to connect with me, to take me up on my challenge, and to show that there's more to him than meets the eye.

"You okay?" I ask.

He wraps his arms around his knees. "I guess so. I just . . . I don't know what I'm doing here."

"So go if you're not comfortable. You don't have to—"

"No," he interrupts, his voice firm with resolution. "I'm comfortable. I am. That's what I don't understand. I shouldn't be comfortable here. Normally, just sitting around would make me feel like I'm wasting time, when I should be taking advantage of every waking moment to advance myself any way I can."

"Glad to hear it." I didn't want to change Gordon completely, strip him of his identity or anything. I only wanted him to relax a little, so this is good. Really good. "Sometimes," I tell him, "I sit here and I'm in a trance. It doesn't matter what's happened during the day, doesn't matter what's going on in the world around me, I just feel calm."

"I believe that's called meditating?"

"Okay. Forgive me if it takes me fifty words to say what takes you one." I laugh. He does too.

I stare out at the water and the ripples on the surface. "But other times," I say, "I sit here and think about people in other places, living lives parallel to mine. Like, maybe some woman in Afghanistan is right at this very moment searching for her missing children, hiding to save her life, while I'm sitting here like a spoiled little princess, worrying whether or not it'll rain today or whether I'll get to keep my motorcycle another year."

"You can't do anything about that woman in Afghanistan, so don't even worry yourself over it. This world needs all kinds of people. You need the poor as much as you need the rich. You need the bad so you can have the good, and you need the unhappy to have the grateful. It's a balance. Like your ecosystem."

"Okay, so who's been cracking open fortune cookies besides me?" I ask.

"It's true." He lies down, arms folded across his chest.

"And I thought *I* was cynical."

"You?" He laughs. "You're the least-cynical person I know."

That's funny, because Rock seems to think otherwise. It's amazing how one conversation with Gordon takes everything I've ever thought and turns it into a pretzel.

"And I'm not being cynical, I'm just being realistic," he says, closing his eyes.

Could he be right? If it weren't for that imaginary woman in Afghanistan, I might not think about how grateful I am. I might be a real spoiled brat, like this one girl Rock was seeing who he kept complaining about. She was never happy with anything. After a while, I finally asked him, "If you're so annoyed with her, why are you still hooking up with her?"

To which he answered, "Because of the sex," scoffing at me like it was the dumbest question he'd ever heard.

Then the horror of that idea stops me. Is that why Gordon's here? Did he incorrectly read my intentions for inviting him? I look over. Gordon seems to be in a state of near slumber, a state I've been in many a time here at the Murphys' dock, so I seriously doubt he is pursuing sexual favors.

"Why do you ride a motorcycle?" he says suddenly. So much for the slumber theory.

"My uncle gave it to me."

"He *gave* you a motorcycle? What is he, crazy?"

"He's dead."

"Oh. Sorry, I didn't know." A moment goes by where neither of us says anything.

"He died of leukemia. Last summer." My words are like little boomerang darts that shoot out, then turn around and stab me.

"What kind?"

"Acute myelogenous." Two words I'll never forget. "He slipped into a coma for two weeks, and then died."

"Sorry, Chloé." He shakes his head.

"No one is sorrier than me, believe me. We were really close, and we built that bike from the ground up. It took us a whole year."

"Ahh," he says. "I get it now."

"He was my adoptive mom's brother," I add.

"You're adopted?"

I nod.

He seems taken aback. "What's that like?"

"Well, I was only a few weeks old when they adopted me, and I grew up knowing this, so I won't find out my life was a lie at thirty."

"Which is good."

"Which is good," I repeat, watching the clouds move in swiftly. "I never really gave it much thought before, but lately, I've been wondering about my birth parents more. What they're like, why they left me, who I look like, all that stuff. Not that knowing those things will change anything— I mean, I love my adoptive parents, nothing will ever change that."

"I don't blame you for wondering. I would too. Just natural, I guess."

"I guess," I say, happy that someone can sympathize. Somehow, it makes this easier.

"I'm sure they had good reasons, though—your birth parents."

"Well, that's what I've always told myself. But still, I just want answers, so I can stop thinking about it so much. Does that make sense?"

He nods slowly. "That it does. Tough stuff. But you're pretty smart to handle it that way."

I try not to smile too much, lest he think I've never heard anybody call me smart before. I don't know why his words send me reeling, but they do. Validation coming from a guy like Gordon can do weird things to a girl. "Thanks."

He clears his throat. "But about the bike . . . aren't you afraid of becoming roadkill?"

I turn on my side to face him, propping my head on my hand. "That is so typical."

"Of what?"

"Of people who've never ridden a motorcycle."

"How do you know I've never ridden one?" I know he can't be serious. He is so bluffing, it's not even funny.

I close my eyes, and the combination of heat and swamp noises starts to lull me. "You haven't, or you wouldn't be asking me that question. Are you judging me again, Gordon?"

"No, I'm only asking because you don't seem like someone who wouldn't care about possibly getting killed in an accident. You seem conscientious."

"I *am* conscientious."

"But people at school see you as this rebel without a cause."

"I don't care how people see me. And just because I ride a motorcycle doesn't mean I'm a rebel."

"Yeah, but how many girls—guys even—do you see riding motorcycles to school? Going against the grain is rebellious by definition."

"Well, I'm not doing it to be rebellious. It's just what I love. It's not a front or fake. Lolita is a part of me."

"Who?"

"Lolita. My bike."

He looks at me incredulously then starts laughing. And right when I think it's over, he keeps laughing. I purse my lips and wait for the hysterics to end. "Oh, man . . . God, Chloé, that's . . . so awesome."

"What? That you laugh at the most mundane things?"

He laughs even harder. "You think it's mundane to give your bike a name?"

"I didn't name her. My uncle did. Can I ask you something?"

"No." He grins.

"This is going to sound strange, but . . . did you cover my motorcycle with a tarp a couple of weeks ago?"

"Uh . . . no. Why?" Judging from his reaction, either he really didn't, or he's a good faker.

"No reason. Someone covered her in the rain the first day of tutoring, but . . . whatever. I should've known you wouldn't do anything nice for me." I give him a playful smile.

"I *might* do something nice for you. You don't have to get all tough girl on me." He tries turning a composed look toward me, but his eyes are smiling. I'd fight back more, but I like seeing him this way. He's a completely different person. I want to take him back for show-and-tell so everyone can see how Gordon Spudinka really is when you break him down.

"Tough girl?" I pick at a piece of rotten wood from the

dock and flick it at him. "Don't be condescending. I am not playing this game with you today." I point my finger right at his nose, but he grabs it and acts like he's going to bite it.

I freeze. Some people are playful by nature, but some you have to encourage, slowly crack open. I look at Gordon smiling, holding my finger—so opposite to how he was in the auditorium today or even the first time I met him. I think I've definitely cracked him open.

And it's sexy as hell.

For the first time since I've known him, I feel hesitation wash over me. Not because we're sitting here with fingers linked, skin and auras touching, but because I don't know how to feel. Half my brain says it's not a good idea to start a relationship while still dealing with the loss of a loved one. If it ends in breakup, it will compound the trauma. But the other half of my brain feels my heart needs this. Something to remind me that life still has good things in it.

Yet here I am in a moment that requires decision making on my part—some sort of momentum—and I can't seem to move. Gordon watches me with his hazel eyes, studying my face, probably wondering what's wrong. I mean, I asked him to come here, and when he finally does, I freak out. Even though I entertained the idea that his wall might eventually come down, I guess I didn't believe that it really would.

But it has.

And because Sagittarius and Leo are both fire signs, well known for being volatile together, and because I'm hardheaded and dive into things I definitely shouldn't be diving into, I brace myself. For the spontaneous combustion that's sure to come.

Eleven

"You know what?" I slip my fingers out of his. "You have to study, and . . . I have to go too."

Gordon's eyes reflect more than just the estuary in front of us. They're loaded with disappointment. I'd love to stay forever, stretching this afternoon as far as it'll go. But I have a chemistry test next Monday to study for, Lolita patiently waits to have her leak fixed, Seth's body slowly withers inside a box, and Rock is probably planting the same lips he kissed me with on someone new. Too much on my mind right now—brain salad.

"Right," he says breathlessly. I could snatch his confusion right out of the air and twist it into a knot. "You're completely right," he says again, only this time, it's as if he remembers he *does* have better things to do. He gets up and brushes his jeans off.

"See you at school?" I ask.

"Yeah. See you at school."

I'm not sure what just happened, but I am glad we decided to ditch tutoring today, even though it probably burned Sabine to see us missing.

Gordon goes back to his car. I get up to stretch. Maybe a buffer comment will help things. "Thanks for following me," I call out.

He raises a hand. I want to hear him say, "The pleasure was all mine, Chloé," but he doesn't.

Try wrapping your mind around ionic compounds when your house sounds like a baby torture chamber and your mom and godmother are arguing over possible reasons for the symphony of shrieks. I watch from the counter.

"It's gas." Mom explains her breast-milk theory for the fiftieth time in the last four days. "I put too much garlic in yesterday's chicken."

"*Non*, Vero, they're just tired." Marraine sets down a Rubbermaid of something she cooked for us and opens it. Is that lasagna I see? Yes! She looks at Baby Carl. "See how his eyes roll back, and that cry—that cry is not one of pain, it's exhaustion."

Papi, smelling of today's catch and the garage again, breezes by on his way into the kitchen. "Have you worked on the leak yet, *hija*? The puddle of oil in the garage is a little bigger," he says above the shrieks. "What about the tune-up?"

"I'll get started this weekend, Papi. I swear."

"Swear, swear . . ." He mumbles something about waiting too long, and don't come crying when I break down in the middle of nowhere, but I can't quite hear due to the twinsies' colic concerto. Even after he grabs his water and heads toward the garage, he's still talking about how "Harleys tend to leak oil . . ." and "responsible ownership of a motorcycle," blah, blah, blah . . .

I cannot think worth a crap in here.

The element symbols jumble around in my mind, forming stick figures that dance in circles, mocking my knowledge deficiency in their jubilation. How does Gordon understand subject matter fifty times more difficult than this in his honors, AP, and IB classes? I try to shake it off and ignore babies Carl and Sagan (ugh), but they just take their screaming to new heights.

I put down my pencil and go to my mom with open arms. "Let me have one so you can eat."

"I'm fine, honey. Marraine's here."

My godmother smiles, and the wild hairs that frame her face bounce around. "Yes, go, Chloé, you need to study. We'll handle the babies."

"You sure?" I ask them. They both nod. I know my mother would love nothing more than to have a five-minute break, and I would love nothing more than to handle my screaming baby brothers instead of studying for chemistry, but they're right—I have a goal. I need to stick to it.

"I'll be in my room," I say, gathering my stuff.

Marraine tries putting Baby Carl in the jaguar-on-a-branch position, face down, draped over her forearm, as

Mom tries the shoulder bouncy-bounce with Baby Sagan, who looks like he's about to pass out from how red he's turning. My mother looks over at me apologetically. "You can help me at bedtime."

I head down the hall to my room, throwing my book and folder on top of my bed. I stop at my computer just to check messages, but end up browsing sites way longer than is reasonably necessary. On one of my mother's zodiac matchmaker pages I select Sagittarius for me, Leo for Gordon, and wait for the analysis. I don't even need to read the whole thing. I already know what it's going to say:

> Wow! Wonderful fireworks always result with these two . . . a sure ten.

See? I knew that already. And it's going to get me into trouble. Especially when your tutor turns out to be hotter than you originally thought. I can't believe this is happening. It's Gordon *Spoonbill*, for God's sake.

I close my eyes and relive the afternoon. Gordon laughing at my joke, his dimples popping out to remind me just how blind I've been for a whole year. His fingers linked around my fingers, making my heart pound in my chest. His face, only a couple of inches from mine.

Studying with Gordon is a chemistry lesson all right. I go back to the zodiac matchmaking page and this time select Sagittarius and Libra, Rock's sign. You know. For self-imposed torture:

> A great sense of comfort, easy communication, and

general well-being occur when you and Libras connect. Libras are a Sagittarius's greatest friends. That's not to say they can't be more . . .

I can't finish. Besides, I've read it all before, how Libras and Sagittarius aren't much of anything at first but can develop romantically over time. I'm about to turn back to studying, when something else occurs to me. I never got around to checking out those adoption agencies last time. So I retype the keywords *Florida adoption agencies* and wait.

Pages and pages of results pop up. My heart rate picks up a bit. I guess the student-tutor line isn't the only line I'm brave enough to cross these days. I start clicking. I read one article about how most adoptions are open or semi-open these days, how adopted kids are keeping in touch with their birth parents, even if it's only through pictures and letters once a year. I don't even have that. The article also mentions how closed adoptions like mine aren't as popular as they used to be a long time ago and how the parents must have had strong reasons to want it that way. That sounds like what Gordon said. Maybe he should've written the article.

One site has a contact page where you type in your information and they'll send you some brochures of information. I stare at the empty text boxes. *It's only to request information, Chloé.* Even Gordon said it would make him wonder. It's just natural to want to know.

Slowly, I type in my name and address, leaving off my phone number. Before I can take it back, I hit SUBMIT and stare at the "Thank You" screen. There, that wasn't so bad. It's not like I am going ahead with an actual search for my birth parents. I just want to see what something like that would cost.

Another article mentions how teens have enough of an identity crisis going on without the added stress of wondering where they come from. It says it's not unusual for kids who previously accepted their history to suddenly become curious when they're teens. Well, they got *that* right.

Mom's knock at the door brings my research to a screeching halt. Quickly, I erase the adoption search in my Google box and close the browser windows. "Yes?"

"Can I come in?"

"Open."

"I can't."

Reluctantly, I roll my chair over and open the door for her. A twinsy has given in to the powerful arms of sleep, cradled against my mother's chest, perfectly angelic, like he wasn't trying out for the Florida Grand Opera half an hour ago.

Mom sits down on the edge of my bed. "How's tutoring going?"

"Going great."

She nods. "You sure? Because if it's not working with this boy, we can get you a real tutor, Chloé. Whatever you need."

"I don't need a real tutor, Mom. I'm trying. Give me time."

"Honey, I'd like to sit and talk with you more, whenever there's a good moment."

About? "I'm always here, Mom."

"No, you're not. You're out a lot and, well . . ." She looks like she has fifty things she wants to tell me but doesn't know where to start. "I know things have been crazy, but let's find the time, okay?"

"For what?" I rub my eyes then refocus them on my book.

There's a moment of silence before she sighs. "Forget it, you're not even listening." She turns around to leave.

"To talk. Yes, I heard you."

But what is there to talk about? I really don't want to discuss Seth's death anymore. We overdid the whole talking-about-it thing when it happened. And yes, I'm having a little trouble in school, but I'm trying to do something about it. What I would *maybe* like to have a discussion about is a subject that may freak her out, given how stressful her life already is right now. But unless she's miraculously learned who my birth parents are and is willing to tell me without hesitation, there's not much to discuss. It'll have to wait until the babies are older and things have settled down.

She looks at me, and I know, from seventeen years' experience, that there's more to this discussion than meets the eye. "Marraine says you've been late every morning for a few weeks now."

"Not every morning. Only one or two." I use my Eyebrows of Innocence to inject doubt into the conversation. Who's she going to believe . . . Marraine or her daughter? *Pfft.*

"Chloé, it's been more than one or two. You need to pass chemistry, and it's your first class of the day."

"I know, Mom!" I start yelling but manage to control my tone right at the end. How did this conversation progress so quickly? The babies have definitely taught my mother the art of time management. "Give me a chance."

Baby Sagan stirs in his sleep. My mother shushes him then whispers, "I am. I just want to make sure you're still on the right track, because I know how easily you can veer off that track if you allow yourself to, Chloé."

"I'm sure this is about me giving up the bike, and you're using my failing class as an excuse. Well, it won't work. Because I'm going to pass."

She sighs. "I never said that."

"You don't have to," I snap. "I know that's your ultimate plan."

She looks stunned. "What? Oh, I see you know everything now. God, Chloé, sometimes talking to you is like talking to . . ." She can't finish.

I raise my eyebrows.

She holds her breath, then lets it out sharply. "Forget it."

To Seth. Talking to me is like talking to Seth. Yes, I know I spent entirely too much time with him and that he rubbed off on me in some bad ways. But he was the most fun of anyone in my extended family, had the most personality, and loved me like his own kid. And he left me his most precious possession, which I'm not about to lose. So I sit up straight, shake off this sleepiness, and focus on passing this stupid excuse for a class.

"Mom," I say, assuming a very studious pose with one hand holding up my head and one hand poised to write. "I'll do it. Okay? I'll pass."

I don't defend myself anymore, even though I know what she's thinking as she leaves my room—that I'm doomed to roam the Earth on a motorcycle like Seth, that I'll never set any long-term goals for myself like Seth. But she's wrong. I do have goals—short-term ones, at least.

Like learning the unlearnable in order to save Lolita from falling into enemy hands.

Twelve

I wake up voracious after a wicked nap. So much for short-term goals. At the kitchen counter, I eat lasagna straight out of a storage container—mine and Rock's servings. My parents are asleep in front of the TV with the babies curled against their thighs. I contemplate taking my brothers to their cribs to give these guys a break, but I don't want to fix what's not broken, so I pluck Lolita's key off the kitchen hook instead.

Inside the garage, the smell of gasoline and motor oil rouses my senses. *There's no better smell in all the world, Chlo,* I hear Sethie say. If Lolita had eyes, she would open them right now, stretch and ready herself for her nightly ride. I flick on the light and see it. A little puddle of dirty oil underneath her. Augh! I am definitely taking care of that this weekend. One more ride is not going to hurt her.

I open the garage and ease Lolita out to the corner stop sign in neutral. The farther away I start her up, the less likely Papi will hear me leaving. I ride away from the low lights of Florida City and deeper into the Everglades, where no one can find me. The sky is even more beautiful out here. As much as I would love to watch the heavens from a strawberry field, there's a state prison right over there, and all I need is for some escaped convict to murder me, then hijack Lolita so he can make his run to freedom. Sometimes I feel like I'm testing fate riding to these remote places by myself, but there's an awesome sense of freedom it gives me that I can't get any other way.

As I drive past Krome Avenue, I look up and see a sliver of moon high in the sky—a thin, turned-up crescent. When I was little, I always told Papi it seemed like the sky was smiling at us. "Yes." He'd smile too, holding in all his pent-up scientific explanations as to the real reason the moon looks that way. "It does, *mi hija*."

My phone vibrates in my pocket. Can't get it now. I take Lolita to seventy miles an hour. For a second, she protests with a cough. *I know!* Lolita rumbles underneath, numbing my legs, my butt, even my arms. Field after field of strawberries and Vidalia onions fly past me, the sweet smells intoxicating me.

There's a path off the road up ahead, near the entrance to the state park where Seth took me one time to see a dead alligator half-swallowed by a giant dead python. I find the path with the moon's help and turn onto it, going down about a quarter mile. When I cut off the engine and coast through the saw grass, all I hear is the rustling of tires over earth. A soft wind makes the blades of saw grass dance on either side of me, as Lolita ticks and cools underneath me. I swerve softly, left then right, swaying like one of them, until finally, I come to a complete stop.

What is Gordon doing right at this very second? Is he thinking about me the way I've been thinking about him? I wish I knew. It would take the guesswork out of everything. My phone vibrates again, reminding me that cell phones and raw nature have nothing to do with each other. In the middle of the field, I dial into my voice mail.

Beep, beep, beep, I press my code, and Rock's voice comes charging into the night. "All right, I guess you're doing something really important. I won't ask what, just use protection. Plus, Amber's having a party on Saturday. Should I go? Chloeee, I need you. Give me a call back, baby doll." *Press nine to save, seven to erase . . .*

He knows about the party.

I consider calling him back, but I'm enjoying the silence too much. Besides, I'm not sure what to say to him. I want to tell him about Gordon and what happened between us this afternoon, yet I know that as soon as I say I like him, Rock's going to make fun and say he's a geek, and that geeks don't care about anybody but themselves. I've heard him talk that way before. Then he'll laugh in a self-conscious way because he knows, somewhere in the depths of his stupid brain, that he only says it because he's jealous.

My phone rings again. I don't recognize the number. "Hello?"

"Hi, Chloé." A guy's voice. Familiar. "Are you busy?"

"Gordon?"

"Yeah."

I stop and catch my breath. "Hey!" I say, totally unable to contain my sudden happiness.

"Listen, I was thinking about some of the things you said today. And well, I kept the paper where you had written your number, so . . ."

I wait for him to finish, but he hesitates so badly. He probably has no clue why he's thinking about me any more than I understand why I'm thinking about him. I empathize. Completely. "I'm glad you called," I say, letting him off the hook. "Where do you live?"

"Live?"

"It's a simple question, Brain Boy."

He laughs nervously. "Why?"

"I'm out anyway. Tell me where you are."

He gives me his address. "But I don't think it's a good idea for you to come. It's late."

"I'll only stay a second, Gordon. I just want to see you. We left on weird terms."

"You sure you want to come over now?"

"Yes," I say before I lose my nerve. "Be there in fifteen minutes." I hang up and look out at the dim landscape. A barred owl flies overhead into some nearby cypress trees. *Am I crazy?* I'm about to head to Gordon's house. At night. After attraction bombs went off between us today. It's becoming less and less surprising that we're acting this way.

But it still makes my stomach flutter just thinking about it.

❁ ❁ ❁

Palmetto Heights is a new home development of affordable mansions with little baby trees still supported by wooden sticks, brick-paved driveways, and sprawling lawns, still unfenced. Half of them are for sale.

I ride by this place every morning on my way to school without really looking at it or realizing Gordon lives there. An omen maybe? Have I been blowing past good things I didn't even know existed? Is Gordon a good thing, or am I being delusional, like Papi selling Mom's garage junk?

I turn into Gordon's street and cut the engine, coasting the rest of the way. I'm sure his mother would completely understand why a leather-clad, five-foot-ten girl would visit her son in the quiet of the night with her obnoxious Harley-Davidson motorcycle. Not!

Gordon's BMW is parked half on the sidewalk behind a Mercedes and a minivan in the driveway. I slide in next to it, blocking myself from the view of the front door, and sit between Lolita and the car. There's a light on in one of the upstairs bedrooms. The blinds are slit open, flickers of bluish TV light reflecting on a wall.

I'm just going to wait here, though hiding in the shadows makes me feel like some creature of the night, stalking its prey. A few minutes go by, and I start to feel really stupid. I should go before I make a fool of myself. But I already chickened out on Gordon once today, and I'm not going to do it again. Whatever happens this time happens.

I close my eyes and listen. A dog barks a few houses away. Someone opens a sliding door and the barking stops.

I also hear some eighteen-wheelers from the Turnpike on the other side of the main road. Otherwise, it's a quiet night.

Suddenly, Gordon's front door opens. Feet shuffle through the grass. My heart pounds in my ears. I better start preparing excuses as to who I am and why I'm sitting here, in case it's Gordon's dad, bringing out a bag of trash or something. Through the darkness comes a rove figure, and for a second, I freak out. It's so dark it really could be Gordon's dad.

But then I hear, "Chloé?" in a deep voice. Finally, I see him clearly. He's wearing drawstring plaid pajama bottoms and a Harvard T-shirt. No socks, no shoes. He looks incredibly comfortable, though something in his face tells me he's just as nervous as I am. Only, he's the one with territorial advantage this time.

"Hi," I say. "Nice house."

He holds out a hand to help me up. "I'll show you around sometime. Just not tonight. My parents are already in bed."

I note the respect in his voice, not only for his parents, but for me as well. I take Gordon's hand and feel his strength as he pulls me toward him with little effort. Our bodies touch slightly. My breath starts to waver. He looks down at me, then his hands cup my face. I let my chin and face go wherever he moves them.

"What are you doing to me?" he whispers.

I want to say the same, that I don't know what he's doing to me either, that I have no idea why I'm at his house right now, that we're clearly very opposite people, and he'd be better off going back with Sabine or finding another SAT-type girl with scores to warrant an entrance exam to MIT like him . . . but I can't speak.

He turns my chin and lowers his lips, softly kissing the corner of my mouth. Then the other corner. I can feel his every light breath. I am powerless to move, and I have to give him points for making my insides melt like this. But this is bad. So very bad. I can't fall for the very person who's supposed to be helping me stay in line. And I am *so* not in line right now.

"Gordon," I say under my breath. *This is not going to work, this is not a good idea* . . .

But he lowers his face again and kisses me for real. So hot and so mind-reeling, I feel like my legs are going to give out, like I've had too much Parrot Bay, except I'm clear as a bell. The only word I can think of is . . . WOW.

Gordon, my peer tutor. I can't get over it. Who knew we could feel this way about each other?

After a minute, he pulls away. His dimples disarm me even in the dark. I lean in and put my arms around him. I smile into his shoulder. *Wonderful fireworks always result with these two . . . a sure ten.* I breathe in the lightly humid scent of his neck and shirt. When I open my eyes, I catch Arcturus and Sirius twinkling brightly in the night. To my left, the crescent moon is still there too, smiling her luminous, silly grin.

And I do the same. Because if the sky is happy, then I'm happy too.

Thirteen

"I have to tell you something, but you have to promise you won't get mad."

Lolita stares at me, wondering why I'm saying this to her when she already knows about Gordon. I sigh and straddle her, laying my head against the handlebars as I wait for Rock this morning. No, I can't say it like that, or he'll think he has reason to be upset, as if I'm in love with him. Which I am NOT.

Ten minutes go by, and no Rock. I take off alone, practicing other ways to tell him that I kissed Gordon, that I really like him, that we should all get together real soon so he can meet him. I decide to ride by Rock's house and see if his car is in the driveway. I come to his corner, afraid of what

I'll find when I turn, and sure enough, another car is there. Even from thirty feet away, I can see this one has an FIU parking sticker on the windshield. A college woman? Where does he find them? How do they find *him*?

I drive off, my stomach feeling like a sack of lead.

If I had a dollar for every quiz Rooney has ever popped, I'd have enough money to buy myself an A. I rip a sheet of paper from my notebook and number from 1 to 4.

"Fold the sheet lengthwise, boys and girls."

I fold my sheet lengthwise. If I'm going to fail, I may as well follow proper format. Mr. Rooney begins writing problems on the board.

> 1. Which of the following compounds would you expect to be most soluble in water?

Lipid solubility? Please, I'm still on elemental compositions. How is one supposed to take a pop quiz on a current topic when one is in tutoring still trying to catch up? They should give students in tutoring a waiver on the basis that they're at least trying. Would it be morally reprehensible to wish that Mr. Rooney would get sick right now? I don't want anything terrible to happen to the poor man, but maybe he could have forgotten to drink his Ensure this morning, so that we might all be excused from this veritable torture. Hello, God?

No such luck. By the time Mr. Rooney has finished writing the four questions on the board, half the class has already found the answers using the book. I am so far behind, I can't even find the answers that way. That's just how "obtuse" the book is, and that's why I want to stick my head inside a paper bag when the guy I switch papers with hands me back a zero out of four.

Merde.

Gordon and I decided to see each other today just after third period, right outside his physics classroom. Won't that be fun? All the geeks, maybe even Sabine, will be staring at me and Gordon smiling at each other like boneheads. Assuming he acts the same and doesn't treat me like he barely knows me, that is.

As I come around the corner, I see Gordon outside the classroom talking to Mr. Phizer. He raises a hand when he sees me. I watch him nod, speak in turn, then shake hands with the teacher. The whole thing is so adult, you'd think he was thirty-five, not seventeen. For a moment, I feel like I'm entirely out of my league. But then I remind myself of what I bring to the table—fun, spontaneity, a sense of humor—and I relax.

Gordon turns with a smile, basking in the glow of his conversation with Mr. Phizer, and heads my way. This is it, the moment Chloé Rodriguez has been waiting for. Will he kiss me again?

I watch his eyes as he approaches. He sees me. He stops. To my surprise, he gently takes my hand. His touch is electric, sending shivers through my body. I lean against the wall, not to look cool but to totally steady myself. The Eyes of Judgment are all around us, especially when he lowers his face and kisses me slowly on the cheek. I try and concentrate on him and only him. He seems really happy today, but nervous.

"How's it going?" I ask.

He sighs big. "Good. I just secured a recommendation for my entrance application, so I'm happy about that. But I still have that big calc test on Monday, which I have to ace."

"Isn't your GPA the highest in our class?" I ask, ignoring some of the stares we're getting.

"Philip's at the top, then Romina, then Sabine, then me. But it's not just this test, Chloé, it's the next test on top of the next test, plus this entrance exam adding to the pressure. It's everything."

"Well, I have something to ask you. And it might help with all the pressure." I bite the inside of my lip nervously.

His eyes hold my gaze. "And what's that?"

"I'd really like it if you came with me Saturday night," I say before I have the chance to remember that Rock wanted me to go with him.

"Where to?"

"A party."

His face loses its energy. "I'm not the party type."

"And what's the party type, pray tell?"

"You know what I mean." He waves his hand around. "There's a whole sect of people who are involved in festivities over the weekends. I know some of you make a career out of it."

"Some of us? What is that supposed to mean, Gordon?" He sounds so clueless sometimes, I have to wonder if he's really all that smart.

We walk down the hall toward his next class. I don't worry about being late to French with Marraine. "I'm just not the party type, Chloé. That's it."

"How do you know if you've never been to one?"

"How do you know I've never been to one? How would *I* know I'm not the type unless I've seen it for myself?" I'm confused. All I wanted was for him to go out with me, but I get this argument.

"Gordon? Yes or no. Will you go to a party with me so I don't have to go by myself and look like a dork, especially since I hate the girl, and she's my best friend's ex, so the whole thing is going to be a little awkward?"

"Was that a complete question?"

I smack his arm. "Yes or no."

He stops just outside his next class. "If I say yes, will you stop hitting my arm?"

I lean into him. Honestly, I don't know where this relationship is headed. Which is probably the real reason I need him to go to this party. If more of what happened last night happens again on Saturday, I'll have a better idea. "Fine, I'll stop hitting you."

He reaches out to brush my hair out of my face—a really bold move, considering the next person who happens to walk by us is Sabine. She's with a friend and slows down to take a sturdy look at us. I fix my own hair so Gordon will take his hand back, and she tears her eyes away, entering the classroom. She looks like she's going to cry. Her friend continues her verbal barrage, unaware of what has just happened.

"Then yes," he says, focusing back on me after seeing

Sabine's reaction. Not that I enjoy seeing Sabine on the verge of tears, but good for him. If it doesn't bother him, then it shouldn't bother me either. "I'll accompany you to your party."

I beam, linking my fingers through his. "Awesome, Gordon. We'll have a grand ol' time. I promise."

"You have to promise more than that. You have a test on solubility on Monday. If you don't promise me you'll study for it, I won't go. I can't have you failing and messing up my transcript." He smiles.

"Okay, I promise."

"You have to study *considerably*, enough to pass it, even if it's only a C."

"I'll try. That's the best I can do," I say. "How about you help me study on Sunday? Then will you go?"

"I've lost track of all the promises," he says. "Let's just go to the party on Saturday, and we'll take it from there."

Yes, good idea. One step at a time. No need to get ahead of ourselves.

"I can't have you failing that class, Chloé."

"Believe me, I know," I say, not mentioning the part about losing Lolita this time. I'd rather he think my actions are purely academically motivated.

The next few milliseconds slow down as he lowers his face and presses his lips against my cheek. "Call me tomorrow," he says, pulling back way too soon, to smile at me.

"Okay." I wish he'd kiss me like he did last night—long and hot, his mouth exploring mine. But we're at school, and this is still very new. He enters his next class, and I'm left touching my hair, smoothing out my shirt.

What is wrong with you, Chloé? You didn't even make out with him this time.

Yet I'm standing here, shaken like a Polaroid by one said Gordon *Spustankoo*. What will people think? I have significant lesbian rumors to uphold! *Par bleu, Motor Girl, get yourself together.* I head for Marraine's class, regaining my composure with every step. By the time I reach her room four minutes later, I'm an indifferent, French-speaking, stargazing biker chick once again.

Fourteen

The laundry situation at home has officially gotten out of control. How can two tiny babies make such a mess of themselves and everybody else? Seriously, our loads have tripled in the last three months. Now in addition to the usual shirts and boxers that need to be hung on the line, there are burp rags, more onesies than are naturally necessary, and even cloth diapers, thanks to my mother's belief that anything convenient must be environmentally toxic.

The only good thing about hanging clothes up outside is that by the time you're finished, you have the same sun-kissed look as after you've just gone riding.

My mother comes out to join me looking strangely

available with empty arms.

"Where are the babies?"

"Asleep."

"And they're not on your chest?"

"Ha, ha." She pulls a waffle-pattern blanket out of the laundry basket and hangs it up. We hang the clothes quietly, and after a minute, she says, "Something came for you in the mail today."

"What is it?" I ask.

"A manila envelope. With an adoption agency's name on it."

Shit. I forgot about that online form I filled out. I pretend to be looking for something really important in the laundry basket. Keep it cool.

"Is everything okay?" she asks.

"Yeah, fine," I say nervously. "Why?"

"Well, it's not every day that you get mail from adoption agencies. Is there something I should know?" Her eyes, the shape of her face, the way she's looking at me, I can't quite read her expression . . . but everything about her makes my heart ache.

"It's nothing, Mom. Probably something Rock signed me up for. He's always doing stupid stuff like that."

"I didn't know he cared so much about your biological origins, honey."

"Mom." I stop her cold. "It's nothing. Don't make a big deal."

She registers the look on my face and her expression softens, but I can just feel the tension between us. This is why I haven't wanted to pursue this before. "Well, if it does ever become a big deal, you can tell me. I won't be upset," she says. "I promise."

My phone rings right at her last word. Talk about getting saved by the bell. "I gotta get this," I tell her. She hands me a blanket with cars and trucks on it and goes back into the house. Good for her for not pressing the issue. These are delicate matters. I'm not ready to talk about this now. I don't even know how I feel about it myself. I never should have filled out that stupid info request.

"Curiosity killed the cat," I answer on the fourth ring.

Rock's voice laughs, smooth and deep. "Bad kitty. What's up?"

"I filled out some online form for info from an adoption place. It came today, and my mom saw it."

"Why'd you fill it out?"

"I don't know. It doesn't mean anything."

"Are you curious about your birth parents? You always said it didn't matter."

"It doesn't. I mean . . . well, what if it does, Rock?" I say, hanging up a tiny sock. "What if something bad were to happen to me like it did with Seth, and there was no one with my DNA to help? What if something happens to my parents? Who would I have left?"

"Me."

"Thanks, sweetie. But you know what I mean."

"Hey, I may as well have no parents either. We'd be in the same boat, you and me."

"Hardly the same thing."

"Is this what you wanted to talk about? You left me a message."

"Uh, no. It was about something else. About . . . my tutor."

"What about him?" His tone changes to worried, serious. What could be more serious than my adoption?

"Well, it's that curious cat thing again. I kissed him."

"You kissed your tutor?" he asks in a hugely exaggerated way. "That's not what he's supposed to be teaching you, doll."

"I like him, Rock. And I'm definitely exploring this, so don't even try and talk me out of it."

"Fine. So you kissed him and found out it was nothing. Next!" he raises his voice to imitate a cashier calling the next in line.

"No, don't think so." I smile suddenly, feeling giddy.

"Chloé, you can't be serious."

"Why not?"

"Because the dude is . . . is . . . Russian."

"So? What does that have to do with anything?"

"It doesn't. I'm just grasping at straws here. Come on, Chloé."

"It's not like I said I was getting married, Rock. Geez. I'm just letting you know what I've been up to lately. That's more than you tell me." Which is probably for the best, or else he'd be informing me of a new girl every other day. No, thank you.

"All right, show's back on. Call me later."

"Hey, Rock . . ."

"Yeah?"

I want to tell him that I saw *yet another* car outside his house, and that I know about the sexual stupidities going on inside, and how I understand they're his reaction to Amber's indecisiveness. I want to tell him that I'm here for him if he needs me, but I'm afraid he'll end up telling me that I can change all that if I would just be with him. "Nothing," I say instead. "I'll talk to you later."

At night, I gaze at the girl in the mirror staring back at me. I'll never know who my face resembles, but some people think I have Mom's body. Tall, thick, no hips rounding out my figure, no hourglass to speak about. My only saving grace from looking boyish is that I have pretty nice breasts. Not too big, they look great in a T-shirt. Did my birth mom look like me? Am I the spitting image of her?

I open the envelope my mom laid on my bed for me. It's some information about making the right choices and feeling safe using Adoption Florida, and a pamphlet about unplanned pregnancy, nothing that would ever help me research who my parents are. White lines of headlights shift across my wall. Gordon is here. I throw the brochures back into the envelope and stuff the whole thing underneath my mattress.

In my boot-cut jeans and T, hair pulled into a tight ponytail, I already look girlier than I usually do, but my reflection seems to want more. *Dangling earrings,* it prods. I never wear them; they bother me when I'm riding, but they would go really well with this outfit. Plus, I think Gordon might like them, so I try them on.

The doorbell rings. I hear my father walk across our old pine floors to answer it. I sit on the edge of my bed and pull on my brown boots, the cute lace-up ones I reserve for nice occasions. I wind up throwing the dangling earrings back onto my junkyard of a dresser going instead with the simple gold studs I've worn since I was a baby.

Gordon and my dad are talking quietly in the foyer. I can't tell what they're saying, but I imagine it's a pretty boring conversation, since my dad knows nothing about entrance exams, and Gordon probably knows nothing about open water-dolphin fishing.

"*Linda?*" Papi calls in a voice that says, "Hurry up, running out of stuff to talk about here."

"Be right there."

I call Rock. I need Amber's address but don't feel like having an issue-filled argument with him right now so I'll have to make it quick.

"Yo," he answers.

"I need Amber's address."

"On the corner of 147th and Florida Avenue. You need it for what, the party? I didn't know you were going."

"I'm only doing it to piss her off. Are you going?"

"Wasn't planning on it, but if you go, I'll go. I have to show her that she didn't get to me."

"But she does get to you. Every time. I hate that."

"I hate that," he tries mocking my voice, but I don't sound that way. "Why don't I just come get you? I have something for you."

"No, I'll meet you there. I still haven't showered," I lie.

"*¡Linda!*" my dad calls again, and this time I hear somebody coming down the hall. It's my mother. She knocks softly.

"I'm coming," I say, right as her head peeks through the door.

"*Mi amor*, Gordon is here," my mother says in her learned Spanish, which sounds as natural as Papi's. "He's very cute, honey. And so smart. It's almost intimidating."

I swivel the phone away from my mouth so Rock can't hear me. "Tell him I'll be right out."

"Chloé, wait. You're not taking that tutor dude, are you?" Rock asks.

"I'll see you there, Rock." I shoo my mother out with a wave. She closes the door. "I assume you'll arrive right at the end, as usual."

"Are you, doll? Answer me."

"Bye, Rock," I say. "See you in a while." I let out a slow breath. He has to stop giving me these guilt trips. I head for the foyer. There stand my dad and Gordon, looking very . . . expectant.

"Hey, ready to go?" Gordon seems relieved to see me. He's wearing the same new shoes as the other day, with jeans and a nerdy Polo shirt, but at least his hair is carelessly tousled, its coolness canceling out the shirt.

"Yup. Let's go."

My mother leans against the wall, watching the scene with a doofy smile, as if her daughter has never gone on a date before. "Don't be out too late," she says. Like I don't go out late every night on Lolita.

"We won't." Gordon smiles politely but doesn't move his feet.

"Let's go," I say again, and I yank him by the sleeve, dragging him out of the house. The door shuts behind us, and off we go.

❉ ❉ ❉

Amber's house is definitely big, a giant Southern colonial built out here when Florida City was nothing but Everglades. It has a wooden front porch complete with columns, swings, and Spanish moss. I half expect the cast of *Gone with the Wind* to be standing there to welcome us inside, but that's where the outrageousness ends. Inside, the place could use a good remodeling.

I lead the way, not really knowing where I'm going. Gordon's hand on my lower back feels nice. It sort of shows we're here as a couple . . . or maybe Gordon's feeling out of place, and this is his security gesture. Either way, it's nice.

"You okay?" I ask over the music.

"Mm-hmm."

We pass PedAndra, who wave at me curiously. I smile at them and scan the room for Rock. Please don't let him embarrass me with some comment about the geek I brought.

"Nice, *chica*," Vince says when he sees me, his eyes roving over my presentation. "Hey, bro, what's up?" he says to Gordon, offering his handshake. Gordon takes it, and I start to feel a little better. Maybe he will blend in. Maybe this will work.

Amber is in the kitchen, blending piña coladas. Vince comes up behind her and pours a shot of rum straight from the bottle into her mouth. Nice. I'm sure Gordon is enjoying watching his party-career theory unfold before his very eyes. I register Amber's expression upon seeing us and smile at her. *If you think this is interesting, wait until Rock shows up and sees you in all your hussy glory.*

When she turns her attention back to the blender, I

mouth, *Where's Rock?* to Vincent. He shrugs, and then kisses Amber's cheek.

"Who were *they*?" Gordon pulls out a stool for me to sit on.

"My friend Vincent and Amber. This is her party." No need to explain the musical chairs going on between them all.

He leans against the wall next to me and surveys the people-scape. There are at least fifty here already, and it's not even ten o'clock. "It's strange how I see these people every day, but I don't really know who they are."

"Well, maybe you could say hello from now on."

"They never say hello to me," he protests.

"Maybe you can be the bigger person and start," I suggest, although it probably won't ever happen. That's just the way things are.

Music blares from the tiny speakers by the computer. Next to it, Alejandra and Pedro are making out as if they're the only people in the room. I make a mental note, that no matter how much I ever have to drink at a party, to always take my hormones outside.

"What do you like about these people?" Gordon asks. I can't even bring myself to get mad at him for saying "these people" again, because he says it so sincerely, as though he really, honest-to-God doesn't understand other walks of life.

"Gordon, open your mind. *These people* are no different from you. They worry, they want to have friends, they want to succeed in life, love . . ."

"But how are they supposed to achieve those things when they're inebriated?"

"They're not always inebriated, dork. They may not have the highest grades, like *someone* we know, but that doesn't mean they go around drinking all the time. In fact, some of them are pretty good at what they do."

Like Alejandra will make an awesome tattoo artist one day, Pedro plays kick-ass guitar, Vince is a successful backstabber, and Amber must be good at *something*, or else Rock wouldn't have wasted so much time with her.

"That depends on your definition of success."

"You're right. And I think success is about being happy."

He smirks. Obviously that is too simple an answer for him. "Chloé, don't be gullible. Yes, happiness comes in many shapes and forms, but for the most part, one needs a certain amount of money to be happy. You need a good job, so you can relax about money, *then* you can be happy."

"Augh," I moan. "You are so complicated."

"And you are so linear."

I eyeball him. "I have been called quite a few things before, but never linear." I watch the people out on the back patio start to dance, thinking about what he said, but I'm not so sure it makes sense to me.

"My parents never argue about money, because they chose a simpler life. Maybe if they'd wanted a nicer house and couldn't afford it, money would be a source of stress, but they don't want that. And neither do I. So maybe there's something to be said about being linear." I shove him in the side with my elbow.

"Ow!" he cries. "Nice rant, and you're right. Lowering your standards can be a good thing, which in essence, is what your parents have done. We could also live off the land like naturists. So then, why are you with me? You could be with any one of these guys." He gestures at Amber and Vincent's friends.

"I could ask you the same thing, Brain Boy." I turn and look him straight in the eye. "If high standards equal happiness, then why are you with me, here, in this cesspool of substandard people?" I wait for the spectacular retort that is sure to come. For the *malevoly* side of him to take over and defend his integrity.

"I didn't mean to piss you off, Chloé." Gordon takes my hand and puts it around his waist, a bold move in unfamiliar territory. I love this side of him. "It was just conversation."

If this is how typical conversations go at Gordon's parties, no wonder he's always stressed.

I'd keep thinking about this some more, but a very familiar person with green eyes and beautiful lips has just appeared to our left. Behind Rock Nuñez, Amber's friends watch him, all worried as though there will be some serious ass-kicking any moment. But Rock's preoccupation is not with Amber and Vince.

Rock looks at me and then at Gordon, and I feel as if time slows down ever so slightly. There's something barely visible in his face—hurt or jealousy—as if Gordon is seriously messing with his property. Then, as quickly as I see it, it's gone.

"Chloeeeeeeee," he cheers over-happily, raising his hand for a high-five.

"Fancy meeting you here." I clasp hands with him and lean in for a hug.

"Yeah, well, I had to see it for myself."

"See what?" I think he means Vince and Amber, but then I immediately regret asking.

"Nothing. Nothing," he says. The atmosphere is loaded with tension. "The party, of course. The beautiful people!" He gestures with wide arms at the room around him.

"Rock, this is Gordon. Gordon, my best friend, Rock." I make sure to add the best friend part to calm Rock down, in case he's thinking of making a fool of himself. I also check the kitchen to see what Amber and Vince are doing. They're pretending not to notice Rock, but it's obvious they're super-aware of him by how blatantly they're avoiding eye contact.

"Bro." Rock takes Gordon's hand in both of his, shakes like they're best buds. Then he pulls out a folded piece of paper from his pocket and hands it to me. "I was saving this for you."

"What it is?" I open it up. It's a page from a magazine. On one side, there's an advertisement on telescopes. On the other is a short article, "Demoting Pluto."

"Saw it in one of my dad's magazines," Rock says. "Thought you'd want to read it."

"This is great. Thanks." I give him my best smile.

Gordon leans in to take a look.

"The de-planetization of Pluto," I tell him.

"De-planetization?"

"Yeah." I don't bother explaining my made-up-word thing. Either he gets it or he doesn't.

"De-planetization." Rock laughs. "Good one." He comes around my other side to reach for peanuts on the counter behind me.

"What's wrong with you?" I whisper. His smile is party

perfect, but his eyes are lackluster. He's not still hung up on all that soul-mate stuff we talked about, is he? As if I'd fall for my best friend, the cliché of all love clichés. Come on, Rock!

"Nothing, baby doll. Why would anything be wrong?" He smiles another fake smile and plants a kiss on my cheek.

"I don't know. Maybe because this is Amber's house, and you guys are off again, and you're nervous that in two point two seconds, you're going to see her and Vince making out." I see Vince nuzzling Amber's neck in the kitchen.

"Hey, what are you gonna do?" He shrugs so casually, I can't quite figure out if he really doesn't care or if this is Rock onstage again. "'Scuse me." He slides past Gordon, laying a hand on his shoulder. "You kids have fun." Then he struts off.

He's overdoing the happy act. Is he mad? I knew coming with Gordon would weird him out, but he has no right to actually be *mad*. Does he ever stop to think about how I feel when he's with a hundred different girls? No, he does not. So he'd just better get over this, quick.

On the counter is a bowl of candy bars. I grab a mini Caramello. "You all right?" Gordon asks, grabbing a Reese's for himself. "You said he's your best friend, but he's not also an ex-boyfriend, is he?"

I laugh a little too loud. "Rock? Oh, God, no, no, no. Rock and I aren't like that. Hell no!" I laugh again.

"You sure? He didn't seem too keen on me being here."

"*Pfft*, please. Rock is never keen on me being with anyone else that makes me happy. I think that's an unspoken rule of best friendship. You know, you never want to see your best friend completely happy without you for fear that he or she won't need you anymore."

"Are you saying I make you happy?"

"Sure, Gordon. Can't you tell?" I give him a sexy smile.

I watch Rock disappear into the party outside, hooting and yelling. The way people respond to him always amazes me. Like the front man of a hot band, he works the crowd and even has his own groupies.

"Let's go outside for a while." I get off my stool and pull Gordon by the hand. "It's getting hot in here."

He follows me outside across the patio, past a human pyramid forming among six people, past the keg and tiki torches, out to a big tree in Amber's backyard. I sit against the tree and start unwrapping my caramel bar. Gordon leans into me, and I stop, chocolate melting between my fingertips, to let him kiss me.

"I've been wanting to do that for days."

"Me too." I feed him a piece of the chocolate. His lips touch my finger and it makes my stomach quiver.

We stay out there for almost an hour, and I forget about everything else except Gordon's words, laugh, and lips against mine. Finally, during one of our long kisses, he reaches a hand around my waist and kneads my lower back. A very primal part of me wants him to reach even further and grab more, but for that, we will have to leave this party. And as if he's heard my every thought, Gordon leans in and whispers in my ear. "Ready to go?"

Fifteen

The road through the Florida Keys is as treacherous as it is lovely. There are a lot more tourists now than when the road was first built, so speed demons used to driving ninety miles per hour on the interstates get frustrated with the slower pace once they hit the islands. It's the silent local welcome. *You're in the Keys now. Slow down.*

Seth saw quite a few accidents along these roads when I was little, mostly involving three-and four-car pileups, with the occasional crushed bike or vehicle careening off a bridge, back when it was one lane each way. The Poker Run, a yearly pilgrimage of thousands of motorcycles through the Keys, always leads to at least a couple of deadly accidents.

So even though the odds are still more in favor of

my getting hit by lightning than having an accident, my parents have always asked that I stay away from the Keys while riding Lolita. But since Gordon's BMW and Lolita are two different species, we head down the island chain on US-1.

Gordon's car is exceptionally tidy inside, except for a few textbooks tossed in the backseat. Between his seat and the center console is a mail package, probably another college application to a ridiculously difficult-to-get-into school. His iPhone is neatly held to the dashboard with an elastic band, as is his GPS. One might psychoanalyze that it suggests a very boring person behind the wheel, but I've noticed it takes a very neurotic person to be so neat. Neurotic people amaze me.

"What do you care about more than anything?" I ask him.

His gaze flits back and forth between the road and the rearview mirror. The reflection of headlights in the mirror outline an eye mask on his face, like a reverse raccoon. "That seems to be changing every day."

"What is it today?"

Five whole seconds of silence.

"You."

"Why?"

His fingers dance on the steering wheel. "I'm not sure."

He's not sure. I stare ahead. We leave the dim lights of Key Largo behind and turn left onto a side road that leads to a private beach. I came here one time with Seth and his friends to catch and release.

Was that unfair of me to ask? Do I even know why I care

about him myself? I don't push it any further, but he goes on. "I didn't mean that the way it sounded. What I mean is, every day for the last three weeks, all I've been able to think about is you. Not that I don't have good reason to. You're . . . amazing." His fingers fly off the steering wheel emphatically. "But I have all these other things that need attention too, and they've been taking a backseat lately."

I pick some lint off my jeans. "I know what you mean. I should be studying for Rooney's test, but instead I went to a party. Now I'm driving around with you."

He raises his eyebrows. "Then I'm a bad influence on you. I should take you home."

I laugh softly. "Gordon, you can't possibly be a bad influence on me, and I don't want to go home." There, I said it. I gulp as quietly as possible. "Where are we going, anyway?"

"Somewhere."

There's nothing down this road except some houses and a bait stand. Other than that, it's all mangroves and fishing spots.

"A place you'll appreciate." He grins playfully.

As we drive in total silence, I realize that if I were in Rock's car, we'd have music on full blast, and we'd be yelling over the noise. But with Gordon, the silence opens up a whole new plane of concentration, allowing me to think about things, like the way we left the party tonight.

He had pulled away from our kiss and pressed his forehead onto mine. And even though I found myself loving the way his voice dropped a couple notches when he said, "Ready to go?," I said, "Not if you have better things to do," because if he thought hanging out at home was more important than being with me, then no. I'd rather stay and hang with Rock. Gordon's eyes were soft, his words, definite: "Then let's go."

I'm really into Gordon, more than I ever have been with anybody, even though I've only known him for a few weeks. But some people just click like that. I could completely fall for him in no time. The truth is, I've been needing to feel crazy-happy for some time now, and he does have some kind of crazy-happy power over me.

Gordon pulls onto a gravelly shoulder and drives slowly until he finds an opening in the mangroves. There's a stretch of beach big enough for two or three cars, end to end. There are lots of stretches like these, where people pull up during the day to fish straight off the beach, jeans rolled up to their knees. But tonight, there's no one.

Gordon parks the car, turns the engine off, and opens his door. *Breathe, Chloé.* I open mine too, the intoxicating salty air hitting my senses. Gordon closes his door and walks around to the front of the car. He jumps onto the hood, which jars me at first. But if he doesn't mind scratching his paint job, then neither will I. I come around and slide up next to him, hugging my knees.

The engine ticks as it cools, but the hood is still hot. Waves creep up, break, and retreat back into the dark ocean. Miami's glow lightens the sky to the northeast. Ahead and to the south . . . black, then even blacker black. The stars are way brighter here than at home. I didn't think that was possible. Orion is super clear. So is Taurus, and of course Cassiopeia, way behind us. Gordon's right, this *is* a place I appreciate. The moon of the other night is nowhere to be found. I miss her smiling reassurance. I look at Gordon's face, nervous and resigned, and realize that he might actually need more reassurance than I do.

I lean back and grab his hand, taking him with me. It's easier to relax when we have something to watch, and the stars put on a pretty good show. "Gordon?"

"Yes?"

"Why are we here?" I know why, but I love hearing Gordon profess, over and over, how he's weakening. I love that I'm responsible for that, that I've broken him down. Everyone needs someone in their life who can tear them away from the mundane. My mom is capable of tearing my dad's eyes away from prime-time TV. I'd like to think that I'm tearing Gordon's eyes away from some textbook right now.

"We're here because . . ." He stares up at the sky for a minute, then turns on his side, propping his head up with his hand. "You love torturing me, don't you?"

I turn to mirror him. His body is way bigger than mine, a nice thing, considering my height. "Yes, but seriously . . . don't you think it's weird? You and me?"

He puts a hand on my hip, and in one steady move, pulls me toward him until our bodies touch. My breathing shallows, my foot shakes nervously. "Not really," he says. "The more I think about it, the more I feel like we should be here. Like fate put us here."

He doesn't blink or flinch or do anything that might indicate he's messing with me. He's serious. I don't know what to say. I didn't take Gordon to be a fate kind of guy.

His forehead touches mine, and his eyes close. I close mine too. "And you believe in fate like that, Gordon?" Rock's million-dollar question.

I can feel his warm breath softly on my face. "Don't you?"

"Yes."

It's true. I do. And a huge part of me wants to dive in and not be afraid of loving him. Maybe I can drown out the sadness of the last few months with something new and powerful. But another part of me says it's too much to think about just yet, to think about it later.

There might not be a later, I can almost hear Seth saying. *Now is what matters.*

But if I get hurt, Sethie? Who do I blame?

"So let's let fate handle this then," Gordon says. I take a deep breath and let his lips touch mine. And it begins.

A very controlled, yet uncontrolled dance, as if some other force is controlling us. It's slow, all hands and mouth, soft tongue and reeling thoughts. Tugging shirts, feeling muscles underneath, his stomach, mine, his hands down my back and up again, in my hair. Beautiful, beautiful, is how I feel. The waves echo our motions, rhythmic, overpowering, but calm, controlled by the tides. I feel the stars pulsing above us even though my eyes are closed. Down, down, we spiral, down a path paved by our instincts, but it doesn't matter anymore.

Because I want this. We are not two different people tonight. We are not Motor Girl and Brain Boy. We are Us. And I don't feel like I just met him anymore. I feel like I've known him my entire life, but that's impossible. Or maybe not. Maybe I have. I'll never know until my time comes and I learn all the answers to this universe. But right now, I want to share myself with him. I want to learn from him, as much as I want to teach him. I want to feel a connection.

I deserve to.

And whether or not those are pheromones talking, whether or not that's the right way to feel, it's the truth.

I deserve to feel happy again.

I never asked for hurt.

Gordon stops and pulls back, his eyes questioning mine. "Are you okay?" He runs his thumb over my lashes, squeezing away tears I didn't even know were there.

"Yeah."

His fingers comb my long bangs away from my face. *It's okay,* his eyes seem to say. And then his warm mouth is back on mine, and the world around us washes into the sea.

Sixteen

Sunday morning, the sun filters in through the same yellow eyelet curtains I've had since I was a little girl. I check my Santa-riding-a-Harley alarm clock. It's past noon. How did I manage to sleep this long without being woken by a baby? My dad must be home to help.

I rub my eyes. And remember last night.

Me and Gordon.

On the hood of his car.

Under the stars, by the water.

The *incredilicious* (incredible-delicious) things that transpired. Without resorting to *full* connection, as a matter of speaking. I smile. *Incredilicious* indeed.

My phone shakes impatiently right off my night table

and onto the floor, but I don't reach for it. I lay very still, thinking. And crikey, do I have things to think about. How am I supposed to study for anything today, much less a class I'm failing, with so many thoughts bouncing around in my head?

Gordon's hands, mouth, body . . . foreign to me before, known to me now. Did Sabine do half the things Gordon and I did last night? Why can't I imagine them like that?

I want to call him, but he might be sleeping. I try to imagine him in his room, and realize I've never seen him inside his house, and suddenly I'm filled with the need to see his inner circle, his house and room, meet his parents. Crazy.

When I check my phone, I see there's a text message from Rock at two in the morning: NEED A RIDE, CALL ME. Crap. 2:03 A.M.? I was sitting in Gordon's car outside my house, saying good-bye. I vaguely remember my phone buzzing, but I was too flighty to remember to check it after our last kiss. I'm sure he got a ride home. Rock does not lack friends.

On my phone, I select Rock's name, pausing to think about what I'm going to say before I press it. What is there to say? That I might be in love? That Gordon's not the loser Rock probably thinks he is, that he's actually sweet and sensitive? Oh, yes, that will go over so well. Sweet. Sensitive. Love. Rock will so enjoy that. Not.

I dial and wait. He doesn't answer. I try again and this time he picks up. "It's about freakin' time."

"Now you know how I feel when I call you for days and you don't answer."

"That's different. I'm a guy. You're a girl . . ."

"Really? I didn't know that."

"I was worried. You need to answer your phone."

"Okay, I get it. I'm a helpless girl. You're a self-sufficient guy. Can we get past it, Grandpa?"

"What's your problem?"

"No problem at all. I'll call you later. Buh-bye," he says sarcastically and hangs up. I call him back, but he doesn't pick up. I call like six more times, and still nothing. His maturity level, or lack thereof, is astounding.

Finally, my phone vibrates. I quickly open it to see a text message from Rock.

shouldn't u be calling ur boyfriend instead of me?

I was just calling u back dork

Not even a minute goes by.

a little late isn't it?

sorry didn't see ur message til now.

of course u didn't. u were too busy w your tooooter

"Tooooter?!" I smack my phone a couple times.

ya, I was busy, is there a problem?

I experience a short wait on this one. My phone buzzes.

none whatso ever.

bullshit. tell me what's wrong.

you like him that much???

why? something wrong with that?

I knew it. I knew he would act this way.

just let it go chlo. let it go . . .

you let it go, freak

Nothing. I wait and wait and try calling again, but nothing. The freakin' nerve! He has no right to be angry with me. He always acts like he's in love with me right after he breaks up with someone. How was I supposed to know he might have really meant it that night at the dock? Besides, *I'm* the one always putting up with him never answering my calls and dodging girls left and right.

"But you don't see me acting all jealous, do you?" I yell at no one.

"Chloé?" My mother calls from her bedroom.

Fudge. "Yes," I mumble.

"Come carry Baby Sagan so I can get some dishes washed, please?"

"Just put him down!" I say impatiently, surprising myself with my tone. I rarely talk to my mom that way. "He has to get used to it," I say nicer. He *does* have to get used to it. Or he'll get spoiled. And we don't want another *Rock* in the world, now do we?

I kick my book bag against my computer desk. I should charge into the garage and take Lolita for a long ride into swampland, especially since I didn't take her anywhere last night. But first, I have to go hold my baby brother. I'll never get to studying this weekend. I close my eyes and breathe *reeaal* deep, counting slowly to ten, purging the thoughts from my brain.

1. Rock, you are a shithead . . .
2. I'm going to fail this stupid class and lose the last surviving piece of Seth I own . . .
3. You're still a shithead, but I feel sorry for you now . . .
4. Gordon, I never imagined you could be this way . . .
5. I can't wait to see you again . . .

6. If fate will allow it . . .
7. A baby is awake and crying . . .
8. Poor thing . . .
9. Let me go and get him . . .
10.

On the floor, my phone buzzes again. My heart starts up
again. I'll just read it, but I won't respond.

> nothing 2 say. we're just frnds u and me, ur not looking
> for anything out of this world, remember????

Grrr . . .

> whatever shithead

Seventeen

I've waited and waited all day. Unless Gordon's phone died, as did his computer, *and* he's being kept prisoner by a group of rabid monkeys, he should've called by now. I need to talk to him so he can explain what relating vapor pressure has to do with concentration of solvent vapor pressure. Fine. I just want to hear his voice.

I eye my phone. *You will ring. Gordon, I know you can hear me. Please call so I know we're okay. I need to know that you're not just ignoring me. Ring . . . ring . . .*

My phone rings. Not.

Siiiighhhh.

So, how do I use the relationship between osmotic pressure and solution molarity to predict the molecular weight of a solute? What's that, Lolita? By purchasing a slice of Ricardo's world-famous flan? How smart you are! Let's go get one, then!

Lolita takes me places. Not just to Ricardo's or school, but far, far away. For example, instead of poring over my studies in my room, she has brought me to the Murphys' dock once again, where I diligently wait for my life to fall into place.

Which maybe I should stop doing and make it happen myself.

But how? I can't make Gordon call me, and I can't all of a sudden become an *intelligoid* and pass chemistry. One thing I *can* do is pull this folded piece of paper from my jeans pocket and see what it is. "Demoting Pluto," the article that Rock gave me last night. You know, when Rock is not being a horse's backside, he can be pretty thoughtful.

I read the article and find it utterly amazing how quickly things can change in this world. We learn things in elementary school that later are disproven, like Columbus not actually discovering America and Pluto going from planet to dwarf-planet status all because less than five percent of the world's astronomers think it should be that way. It makes me wonder: why should we get used to anything when nothing is permanent? Even people. Why should we put our hearts way out there for them when they're only going to die on you one day?

In the grand scheme of things, that may be a pretty stupid way to think, but it's true. Why should we invest our time and our energy in people if ultimately, they're not going to stick around? Case in point: Why would I set myself up for more hurt by trying to locate my birth mother? She didn't want me then; she's not suddenly going to want me now. Is my need to satisfy my curiosity important enough to put up with that?

I think it may just be.

In the distance, dark gray clouds slowly roll in. The wind picks up, and the saw grass performs a blustery ballet. No matter how hard I try, I cannot get into this stupid chemistry book. I keep reading the same paragraph over and over. My caramel flan did not inspire me as well as I'd hoped it would. I try calling Rock again.

"Yes?" He answers, voice husky and full of sleep.

"Uh, hi, is this the immature oaf who can dish it but can't take it?"

"That depends. Is this that sexy biker who thinks her tutor is the answer to her nightly prayers?"

"We only went to the party together, Rock. Big deal." I can totally imagine him on his back in bed, arms behind his head. What if there's someone with him?

"Only the party? Is that why you didn't call me back until this morning? Who do you think you're fooling, Chlo? Besides, you were looking more dolled up than I've seen you in a while. I may be stupid sometimes but not *that* stupid."

"Fine. Maybe I do really like him. But what sucks is that I don't feel I can tell you that. You're changing our dynamics, and I don't appreciate it."

"You can tell me anything. You know you can."

"No, I can't. Because you'll get jealous, and you'll say things to embarrass yourself."

"Why don't you try me? You haven't even given me the benefit of the doubt."

I sigh into the phone. "Okay, let's try it. Gordon is not the selfish geek you think he is. He's incredibly nice to me, even though we argue sometimes. He's different, and I like him. There." I wait.

"Different. Right. Mm, hmm." I hear his TV on in the background, and his low, reassured laugh. "That guy doesn't care about you the way you think he does, Chlo. Guys like him . . . something always takes precedence. But keep talking . . . you're cute when you're naïve."

"See? I knew you couldn't do it. And you're not one to talk. All you ever date are sluts like Amber."

"Uh, I *want* sluts. I doubt, however, that you are actively seeking assholes."

"How do you know he's an asshole?"

"See, you admit it."

"Augh! You're being judgmental. Some might say *you're* an asshole."

"I don't care what *some* might say. Would *you* say that?"

"No," I say quickly. I wouldn't. Sure, Rock might be hard for some people to take, but once you realize that he's not mistreating anyone and that the girls he hooks up with are just as interested in him as he is in them, it's hard to call him an asshole. He's not deceiving anybody, and the only person I can think of that he's ever hurt is himself.

"Well, I'm glad to know I still have your loyalty," he says. "But if you ask me—"

"Which I have not . . ."

"You still shouldn't be seeing that dude. You should be with me. Because at least you'll know where you land on my list of priorities—numero uno, baby."

"Of course you'd say that, because you're incorrigible."

"Thank you, and you're hot."

"Shut up. When are you going to help me fix that leak already?" I ask, changing the subject.

"Whenever you want. I'm always here."

"Yes, but never alone, so you have to come to my house."

Suddenly, I hear gravel crunching behind me, back on the road. I sit up quickly and turn to look. I see Lolita, but nothing else. The grass and bushes block my view.

"What are you doing?" Rock asks, yawning.

"Nothing. I gotta go."

"So go," he says.

There's definitely a vehicle back there. My heart speeds up a bit. Nobody ever comes out here. Could it be Gordon? "Rock, I'll call you back."

"Later." He hangs up.

I close my phone and stand to get a better look. "Hello?"

A car door slams shut. Feet crunch over the pebbles, and for the first time, in all the time I've been coming here, I feel unprotected. Suddenly I feel stupid for hanging up with Rock.

"Hello?" a male voice calls back. "Who's there?" A man appears from around the tall grasses in a red polo shirt with some white lettering and a logo, pencil over his ear. Who dares invade my sanctuary?

I don't answer. My heart pounds in my ears. He looks twentysomething, brown hair underneath a baseball cap with a county patch on it. "You okay?" he asks, looking around like there might be someone with me.

"Yes. I'm just doing homework," I say, pointing to my book. Why did I tell him that? I don't have to explain myself to a stranger.

"Is that yours?" He gestures to Lolita.

"Yes."

Pause. Confused look. He nods, checks Lolita out, then looks back at me as if trying to match the rider with the bike. He shrugs. "Cool. We're just going to measure out here. You don't have to go anywhere."

"Measure what?"

"The property, the easement, the whole lot."

I get a sinking feeling in my stomach that ends in a tight knot. "For what?"

He turns and looks at the Murphys' old house with its broken windows and leaning chain-link fence. "This is coming down. It's all going to be razed and rebuilt."

"What do you mean? Why?" Who would want this land in the middle of nowhere?

The county worker looks annoyed with me now. I guess it shouldn't come as a surprise that someone wants to move here next to the estuary. I try to imagine who might've seen this area on a map and decided they like it as much as I do. Have they even been here to check it out? I've never seen anyone. "It was auctioned off. You won't be able to hang out here too much longer. We'll probably get started soon."

"What?" I ask, hearing panic in my voice. Where am I supposed to go? This is *my* place! "Who bought it?" I demand, feeling sick.

"The county? A private owner? I don't know who. I'm

just here to survey." He waves, indicating the end of our conversation and heads back to his truck. More voices come. More men to steal my dock with their measuring tapes and clipboards.

I can't believe this. No one has cared about this place for years. I look at the water, trying to imagine a new family moving onto this land, completely tearing down the Murphys' house to build another McMansion complete with patio and dock. I will no longer be welcome here.

"How long do I have?" I call out, but the man has headed toward the other side of the property. The clouds are almost overhead now, the humidity already sweetening the air. *Time to move on*, the clouds seem to say. *Time to go.*

But I won't.

I've already been asked to let go and move on once this year.

This is my place, my refuge. So if a bulldozer has to run me over and then scrape up my flattened body to get me off the property, so be it.

Eighteen

Test Day.

Problem is, I can't stop thinking about the Murphys' dock coming down. I can just see the wooden planks splintering into a heap of junk underneath metal jaws. I feel violated, the way Mom might feel if my birth mother suddenly came careening into our house, demanding she wants me back. Would she have the right? After Mom has loved me more than anyone else?

The memories of Saturday night's bliss don't help either. I try to focus, shake off the thoughts, but Mr. Rooney's clock ticks painfully loud, and I can't concentrate on anything I'm supposed to.

Mr. Rooney wears his pink lab coat today. He resembles

upside-down cotton candy on a paper stick with his white hair all sticking up in the back like that. Also, because his eyesight is dusty, he has chosen Alejandra as a lookout, which means she'll take her test when we're finished. She sits on a special stool, vigilant and indifferent at the same time. She is a minor geek, meaning she is the smartest in the class but still has friends and a reputation to think about, so she really has no intention on ratting out any cheaters. Pedro makes sexy faces at her to try to make her laugh.

On my test, the hieroglyphics laugh at me. *Ha!* they say. *You're funny, Chloé Rodriguez, to think that you could attend a party, have a near-sex experience on the hood of a car, ride Lolita most of Sunday afternoon, and* still *believe you could pass this test come Monday morning. You silly girl!*

Some of the hieroglyphics do not laugh. Some of them like me and present themselves as comprehensible to my puny brain, but there aren't enough of them, and I will certainly plunge to my academic death after today. But I won't tell my parents. I will find a way to make up this setback, even if I have to wear a tiny lab coat, knee socks, and pigtails to get on Rooney's good side.

Gross. I cannot believe I just thought that.

Still, if I have to, I will.

I rush out of Rooney's and let out a giant sigh, then I bolt down the stairs toward second-period English. But instead of turning right, as usual, I turn left, taking the long way so I can avoid Marraine's classroom. The last thing I need right now is Marraine asking me how the test went.

In the hallway, I pause to lean against the wall and let the facts slowly sink into my consciousness. *You have one and a half grading periods left to pull that grade up to a C.* Which means I'll have to get an A or B on every test for the next four months if I want to keep Lolita. Every test!

I am doomed like a duck at a croc's dinnertime.

I see Amber blazing down the hall in a huff. Trailing her is Vince. He catches up with her and tries putting his arm around her shoulders, but she elbows him in the ribs. Ouch. Trouble in paradise already? I scan the hallway for Gordon. Will he be back to the old Gordon, acting like I'm a waste of his time? I have to wonder, since he didn't call me yesterday. My heart is doing flips, cartwheels, roundoffs, *and* backsprings, just thinking about it.

I kick off the wall and quickly head to my class. Then I see Gordon, talking to Ms. H in Hallway A. She nods and smiles at him as he speaks. It amazes me, the effect Gordon has on the faculty. Does he even have to try at all? Or does he always have carte blanche?

I stand against a column, prepping myself for when he turns and notices me. I'll smile and wait. The ball is in his court.

Ms. H pats his arm—*good boy*—nods some more, and gestures to her class. She waves bye-bye and disappears inside. Gordon smiles, clearly pleased at another successful teacher-student interaction, then looks at his watch. He turns and starts walking in the opposite direction from where I'm standing.

"Psst," I beckon him.

He looks over his shoulder with this madman-on-a-mission face and slows down. Something about the way he does it makes me feel like I'm keeping him from more important things. I push that idea aside.

"Hey, Chloé," he says, running a hand through his hair. He gives me a weak smile. "I'm sorry I didn't call you yesterday. I got tied up at home."

"That's okay. I know you have your calculus test today."

"Yeah." He pauses uncomfortably.

Are you going to mention Saturday night? We kind of bared our souls there, Gordon.

"What about your chemistry test? How did you do?" he asks.

"I think I did all right. I studied on my own yesterday, so we'll see."

He smiles, nods, looks around the emptying hallway. The electronic bell whines above us. No kiss, no going for my hand. *Earth, swallow me now.*

"That's great. Maybe you won't need me anymore, huh?" He laughs, but that's not funny. Why wouldn't I need him anymore?

I try to speak with my eyes and tell him that the other night meant something to me, that it wasn't just another day in the life of Chloé Rodriguez, and that I've never felt that close to anyone before, that I want to see him again. But it's not working. I'll have to use words. "No, I think I still need you . . . actually."

His smile dies down. This is it. This is where he tells me that Saturday was a mistake, that we are not a couple, he just had an episode of temporary insanity. I'm a distraction to his agenda.

"Ladies and gents . . ." Our security guard strolls down

the hall, wagging her walkie-talkie around in the air. "Move along. Let's go."

"I'll walk with you," Gordon says, flanking me as I hurry away.

"Gordon, just . . . don't. You know? I was on my way to class, that's all. It's okay if you're having second thoughts. I understand."

"That's not it, Chloé. But I can't make it to tutoring today. I have a paper in literature, and a test in calculus . . ."

But doubt still lingers in his eyes. I can see it.

He reaches for my hand, and my stomach takes a dive. "Look, I have to go right now. I only have two periods before my calc test and I should do some last-minute studying."

"Of course," I say, but my mind has other ideas. *Come on, abandon protocol like you did the other day and cut class with me.*

He stands there, playing with my fingers, and finally reassurance settles over me. His hazel eyes plead with mine. He did feel it the other night, didn't he? Just like I did. It wasn't nothing to him, and I didn't scare him away. His hand gently lifts my chin, and his face slowly meets mine.

It's the kind of kiss that makes you forget where you are. It's so powerful, I wonder how this could possibly be anything but right.

I pull away, get my bearings. "Go, call me later. You know, if you can."

He's not leaving. His gaze is fixed on my face. Wheels are turning in his head, and I can tell he's breaking down. There comes a time when nothing can interfere with your body and heart or what they tell you. And from the way Gordon won't move, I realize that now is one of those times.

"What's up?" *You can't go to class, can you? I know. I feel the same way.*

He pulls me along gently. "Come."

"Where we going?"

But Gordon doesn't answer. I try to imagine how we must look together right now. Gordon, six foot four and unaware of his hotness, tugging this boyish girl with wild auburn hair behind him. We don't match and yet we do, and that's what's so beautiful. I'm so flustered, I hardly notice Marraine walking opposite of us, eyes carefully processing. Shit, I forgot about her planning period.

"Bonjour, Madame," I say quietly, avoiding her eyes.

"Bonjour," is all she says, not that I need more words from her to know what she's thinking.

"That was a good accent. I take it you have Madame Jordan for a class?" says Gordon.

"Yes, but she's also my *marraine*—my godmother."

He looks at me. "No way."

"Yeah."

"Wow."

"Tell me about it. This will reach my mother's ears in no time."

That doesn't distract Gordon from his mission—to take me out of here. Where, I have no idea, but I'm so out of my element, I feel alive. And believe me, after the way I've been feeling for a while now, that's a very good thing.

❖ ❖ ❖

Twenty minutes later, we are in the last place I would have ever imagined: Gordon's house. His parents are at work and we are alone in his room, which is as straightforward as his car. Desk, super-organized. Computer, clearly an expensive buy. Nothing on the walls, except for a small chart of the periodic table near his desk.

"Why would you put this up?" I laugh. "Don't you get enough of school at school?"

"I put it up last year, and I guess I just left it. I don't even realize it's there anymore."

It amazes me how Gordon is my same age, same grade level, yet in some ways, he feels so much older, it's sick. I try to suppress my feelings of academic inadequacy. I scan the room for any posters, pictures of Sabine he might still have around, anything. There's a lamp and remote control on his night table, and a bunch of DVDs strewn about, but otherwise, not much.

"Have you ever skipped class before?" I lay on his bed and watch him pick the DVDs off the floor.

"All the time, but I usually skip to other teachers' classes. To study. My teachers never care."

"But not for going home, right? Not for being with a girl."

"No, not for coming home."

"Then you're becoming more like me," I tell him. "That must scare the crap out of you."

"You have no idea."

I gasp. "No likey!"

He chuckles, lying on the bed next to me, taking my hand in his. "Yeah, but you're becoming like *me*, too. Studying, acing tests . . ."

"I never said I aced my test," I remind him, swallowing my dread. *God, he really thinks I did well.*

"So maybe we're meeting in the middle somewhere."

"Maybe we are," I say, moving closer to him. I want to feel his arms around me. But I'll wait for him to make the first move. How far do I want to go? Am I ready for this?

"Maybe that's how couples are to supposed to be—flexible."

So we are officially a couple, straight from the know-it-all's mouth. I refrain from doing little cartwheels in his bed. "Maybe."

He stares up at the ceiling. "Maybe I need to get my butt back in time for the calc test at one o'clock. Maybe we're full of shit, and coming here was a huge mistake."

I close my eyes. "Maybe we should stop saying 'maybe.'"

"How are we supposed to know, Chloé?" Sexy, full mouth, tinged with uncertainty. Stubble, so hot.

"We're not. We're supposed to figure things out as we go along."

"Typical Chloé answer. Fortune-cookie queen."

"You're mean." I press my forehead into his.

He laughs, and I may be mistaken about this, but he seems almost pleased with that, like he likes being called mean.

"Gordon?" I take his hand and feel the smoothness of his nicely squared nails.

"Motor Girl?"

"I'll ignore that."

"Why? That's who you are. You said so yourself. You love riding Lolita. It's not an act."

"You're right, but I hate that people who don't know me call me that. Like Sabine when I first talked to her in tutoring."

"Maybe she thought you were proud of it. *I* thought you were proud of it."

"Why would you?"

"Well, because it's not really an insult. It's a name based on observation."

"I guess you're right. Speaking of Sabine," I say, playing with a piece of thread to keep my eyes off him. "Did you guys . . . you know."

He shakes his head. "No. We were together for a few months, but nothing like that ever happened. Which is probably why my parents liked her—still like her. But last year, before I moved here, I had a serious girlfriend in Boston. And . . . yeah."

"Ah, sorry I asked." My mind conjures up an image of Gordon and another girl naked in bed, having experiences I haven't had yet.

"Don't be." He presses his hand against mine. His is much bigger. "What about you? Have you ever *been* with anyone?"

I shake my head.

"Never?"

"Geez, don't act so surprised, Gordon. We Motor Girls are sensitive creatures."

He's quiet, thinking about things. I watch him blink every so often, the tips of his lashes glowing from the light coming in through the window. I bite his fingertips and wait for the words to spill from my lips. "You're so focused. I wish I could be more like you sometimes."

"No, you don't. Trust me."

"Yeah, I do. I wish I could balance life out more and focus on school the way you do." I want to tell him more about the way I feel, but I'm scared to. What if I end up pushing him away instead of bringing him closer? I decide to risk it a bit. "I care about you, Gordon. A lot."

He links his fingers through mine and presses my hand against his face. I love the way it feels. "Of course you do," he says, trying to hold in a laugh.

"Wha—you egomaniac!" I hit him in the arm and chest.

He lets out the laugh and rolls me onto him so easily and smoothly, it makes my limbs weak. "I care about you a lot too, Chloé. Do you think I'd be here with you if I didn't? The truth is, no one has ever made me feel this way before."

"No one?" I raise my eyebrows. *Not even Sabine, nor his girlfriend in Boston?*

"Nope. Not like this."

"That makes two of us."

"It feels dangerous. The way I could easily fall for you."

"That it does."

His eyes flit across my face. "You know, you're really beautiful. I mean, I always knew you were pretty, but I'm looking at you now, and man . . ."

"What?"

"Amazing."

I've never been one to blush, but this would be the moment to start. "Wow, Gordon. I don't know how to react to that. Thank you, I guess."

"Don't thank me. It's true." He kisses me, softly at first, then it turns really hot. Slowly, as if gauging whether or not I'm up for repeating Saturday night's episode, his hands slide through my hair, down my arms, and then to my breasts for a moment. Suddenly I feel like I do when I'm taking Lolita for a ride on an open road in the middle of the Everglades—nothing ahead of me, nothing to stop me, no road signs, no cops, no parents. Where I go from here is entirely up to me.

My mother's words *dangerous* and *reckless* slide out of my consciousness and try to warn me. But as I also do when I'm on Lolita, I push them out of my mind and prepare for the adrenaline rush ahead.

Nineteen

Throughout February, it feels like someone has lit a bottle rocket inside my soul. Right through our standardized testing and February's romantic activities, I can't think of much else except the next time Gordon and I see each other again. Even my last test, which I failed. It's getting more and more difficult to focus during tutoring, but I'm still going. It's the only time I can be sure to see Gordon at school. Otherwise, we see each other at the dock, whenever we can sneak into his house during the day, and at my house on weekends.

My parents love him. Of course they do. How could I have landed such a responsible young man as this? Rock, however, is a different story. Gordon and I have been together seven weeks now, but Rock still treats him with much the same indifference as I showed Amber. As if dating Gordon and dating Amber are anything alike.

From time to time, I still think about Rock's comment about how Gordon would always have higher priorities than me. When it comes to study time, yes, he's pretty disciplined. And also during the day, because he needs to stay focused during school hours, but after school, he's pretty much all about me, with nothing to interrupt us. My only complaint is that I still haven't met his parents. I know they're strict, so I haven't pressed the issue, but still, it would validate our relationship in a huge way.

On St. Patrick's Day, we forgo any festivities and just hang out at the dock, which, thank goodness, is still standing. Our heads touch, our fingers link, nice and tight. I feel like I'm on the edge of something, but I don't know what.

Most of the stars are covered by a thick stretch of clouds tonight. I focus on one very faint star just within the cloud cover. "Do you think there's life on Gliese 581c?" I ask, pretending it might be the faraway planet itself.

"Gliese 581c?" Gordon brings my hand down to his chest and lays it flat.

I turn to him. "You mean to tell me that Brain Boy doesn't know about the planet in another solar system that might possibly have the same watery conditions as our own?"

"I knew about it. I just didn't know it was called Gliese 581c." His smiling voice resonates in the chirpy night. Add to the crickets a light breeze and saw grass rustling, and this is a beautiful lullaby of a night. "Couldn't they have given the thing a better name? I mean, Earth isn't called 'Sun 14b.'

It should be, like, Magnus or something."

"Right? Or 'Ratatooey,' or 'Bunsolar,' or even 'MegaPlanet' would've been better."

He laughs quietly.

I smile and close my eyes. I wish this night could last forever. His shirt smells like his room, a smell I've come to associate with some pretty interesting goings-on. Everything except the final deed, that is. For that, I've been waiting for the moment when I realize I love the right person—and after almost two months, that time has pretty much arrived. Because it does not get any better than this right here.

The clouds move away, exposing the sky again, and the stars sparkle like a glitter-on-black-construction-paper project I made back in fourth grade. I remember I added little aliens to mine, and my teacher gave me a happy face with antennae on it. "Do you think there could be aliens living there?"

Now he'll argue about what aliens really are, or suggest that *we* are the aliens. Watch.

"What I'm more concerned with are aliens living here. *Inside* our planet even." He holds up a professor-ish finger. "Have you ever noticed that the North and South Poles are always covered with clouds in satellite images?"

I narrow my eyes at him.

"For real. There are huge holes at the poles. Holes that could lead to a whole new world inside our planet. You didn't know that Earth is hollow?"

I stare at him dumbfounded. He sounds so serious, I can't tell if he's kidding or not.

He chuckles softly. "That's what some people think, at

least. Hollow Earth theory. I can't believe you don't know about that, you of astronomy interest."

"No, that is definitely a new one for me. I'll be sure to research it, as soon as I get home." I laugh.

"Do you really research stuff when we're not together? I thought all you did was ride Lolita or talk with Rock."

"You know," I say, clucking my tongue, "you have this way of being completely honest yet insulting at the same time. It's so innocent, it's endearing."

He smiles, eyes closed.

"To answer your question—yes, I really do research stuff."

"Like what? Give me an example."

I sigh. "Well, whatever's on my mind, really. Lately, it's been adoptions. Like how so many people are against closed adoptions nowadays. They make up, like, two percent of all cases. Most people think it's really cruel for the adopted kid to not know anything about their parents."

He turns to look at me. "How do you feel about it?"

"Not sure." I shrug. "I don't think it's cruel. Had my adoption been open, it would've been weird to always see my birth parents, knowing that they're available yet I can't be with them. I think that's more cruel than not knowing who they are."

"And if you do come into contact with them, there's no guarantee that you're going to like what you see."

"Yeah, like this one man I read about whose birth mother used a private investigator to find him. She started stalking him to the point that the man had to put a restraining order on his own birth mom. That's messed up."

"Yes, but it's one extreme case, Chloé. Are you going to go through with it? An investigation into your case?"

Hmm. The billion-dollar question. "Right now, I think I'm leaning toward yes. I know that I might find some sad woman who doesn't want anything to do with me, and I know that she could also have a litter of kids, which might make me feel like crap that she kept those but not me. But the thing is, I just want to see her. I want to connect, then get it over with. Assuming she's even alive."

"I get it. For closure."

"Exactly."

"Are you going to tell your mom?"

Pfft. The trillion-dollar question. "If there is a way for me to do this without involving her, that'd be awesome. But I don't know if there is."

We're quiet for a while as he plays with my fingers. It's weird to be thinking about all this adoption stuff. A year ago, none of it would have ever crossed my mind. Today, I'm seriously considering it.

My phone vibrates inside my jeans. I pull it out and see it's Rock. I put the phone back into my pocket. I've learned to keep Rock and Gordon in separate corners, and right now, I'm giving Gordon my full attention.

"Who is it?"

"Rock."

"Are you going to answer it?"

"Nah, he just wants to know what time he can come over and help fix Lolita's leak," I lie. He probably wants to see if I'm here so he can join me. "She's long overdue for a tune-up, too. Poor thing needs some TLC."

"The bike or Rock?" he asks.

I'm shocked into silence. I swallow a ball in my throat. "What do you mean?"

He shrugs like he shouldn't have brought it up. "Nothing. I just thought maybe our being together has put a strain on your friendship with him."

"We're good. We're fine," I say, but it sounds forced even to me.

"If you say so," he mumbles.

I realize it can't be easy having a girlfriend with a best friend who's a guy, especially a chick magnet like Rock, but Gordon has taken it pretty well. Then again, he is the most mature seventeen-year-old I've ever met. "Babe?" I ask.

"Yeah." I love the vibrations his voice makes against my hand on his chest.

"This might sound stupid—and with the way you overanalyze every little thing I say sometimes I'm even afraid to say it—but since today makes seven weeks since we first kissed . . ."

"Good God, woman, spit it out!" he cries.

I laugh nervously against his shirt. "Okay. I just want you to know that I really love you. And that I respect you. And that you're adorable to me. Like, really adorable, if that makes any sense. Seriously, I look up to you." My chest feels tight as I say this. "You've given me immense amounts of faith that I can do better, and for that, I just want to say thanks."

He clears his throat. "Wow, Chloé, I appreciate that. I really do."

I sigh, happy that I could finally tell him how I feel and that he seems okay with it.

"But I'm sure you know . . ." he goes on, "that *adore* means 'to worship,' and . . . you shouldn't worship anyone. Not even me."

I push myself up to get a good look at him, but it's dark, and all I see is his outline. "Whoa. Chill, Brain Boy. I didn't mean it like that. All I meant was that I admire you, which is a good thing. And that I've changed since being with you. I think the person you're with should make you a better person."

Don't you think so? I'm dying to ask, but I will not lead any witnesses today.

"And I agree," he says. "Just making sure."

Whew! I lean forward to kiss him. "Don't worry, I don't have any secret statues of you in my closet. And just so you know"—I mimic Darth Vader's notorious line— "I find your lack of faith disturbing." *Let's see who the geek is now.*

He side-glances me in confusion.

"*Star Wars*," I say.

"Ah. That shouldn't surprise me," he mumbles.

"What," I say, acting shocked, "does that mean?"

"It means"—he brushes my hair out of my face and kisses me softly—"that I should stop underestimating you."

Marraine once told me that you can look into a guy's eyes and see if he's lying or not. If he flinches or looks away, don't trust him. But Gordon's eyes are steady. Strong. As steady and strong as I can tell in near total darkness.

"Thanks, sweetie."

"You're welcome." He kisses me again, then pulls away quickly. "And going back . . . no, I don't think there's life on Gliese 581c."

"And why not?"

"Because it takes a lot more than just water to re-create the exact atmospheric conditions as Earth's. It takes carbon dioxide, and nobody even knows if either exists there. Besides, half the planet faces its star all the time, so it's scorched."

"So . . ."

"And the other half is permanently in the dark, so it's too cold. Not exactly suitable for life, is it?"

"Is everything always so black and white with you? What about that buffer zone in between? That twilight zone that's sort of in the star's light but sort of out of it at the same time? Could there be life there?"

Gordon ponders this. I'm curious to hear his answer. If he thinks like I do, he'll think it's possible, and we should probably send NASA over there sometime soon to find out. If he doesn't . . . well, then he'd be the first nerd I've ever known to think that other worlds don't exist.

"Are two human fingerprints the same?" he says. "In all the six-and-a-half billion people in this world?" He presses my fingertips, one by one, with his. "No, they're all different. So I think Earth is doomed to be unique, a fluke of nature, kind of like us. And speaking of freaks, we both know there can only be one Chloé in the world, right?"

The punch comes hard. Right into the center of his tricep. But he's learned enough to laugh as he's crying out in pain. I know I'm right about the twilight zone on Gliese 581c, and life could so totally lurk there. And as he stares out into space, I find that I am not staring at the stars like I usually do. I am staring at him.

Maybe he's right. Maybe in some weird way, I do worship him. But is that such a bad thing? *Only if he can't empathize,* I figure. *If he doesn't know what adoring someone feels like.*

My phone does a short buzz, indicating I have voice mail. I call in to listen.

There's one message, two minutes old from Rock. His voice sounds low, borderline depressed. "Happy St. Patty's Day, Chlo. Call me if you want." And the guilt I feel for spending all my time with Gordon stretches from here to Gliese 581c.

Twenty

Every so often my dad goes fishing, not for a paycheck but purely to get out of the house. Two weeks later, the moon is full, and Papi decides it's time to go out. Moonlight fishing is not the best for catching anything, but for catching sleep, it's priceless. Usually, he goes alone, but tonight, he's invited me along. Since Gordon is working on a project anyway, I take him up on his offer.

Our boat gently rocks somewhere near Sugarloaf Key on the Gulf side. Lying on my back, I watch the moon to the east get surrounded by clouds never thick enough to completely cover her. Papi sits on the other side of the boat, setting up his line, a cold beer between his knees. He doesn't say much, just strings up his lures and sinkers.

"What are you going for tonight?" I ask.

"Whatever bites," he says. "Snapper or tarpon probably."

"Tarpon? Yuck." I close my eyes and imagine coming out here with Gordon sometime. We could probably get into a lot of trouble alone on a boat with the way we're always heating up. I wonder what he's doing right now.

"So, *linda* . . ." Papi sits back, spreading one arm along the side of the boat, holding his beer with the other hand.

"So, Papi . . ." Here comes the interrogation. I don't mind his because they're always so annotated. Plus, I know he trusts me completely, always has.

"How's it going with chemistry?"

"Chemistry is fine."

"Rock?"

"Fine."

"Boyfriend?"

"Fine."

"Using protection?"

"Don't need it yet."

"That's my girl." He takes another swig of his beer.

I smile at the moon. Jupiter plays peekaboo between the cloud cover, just about the only star visible tonight. I curl up on my side, closing my eyes, feeling the ocean rock me to sleep.

"You don't know why we're here, do you?" he asks suddenly.

My eyes shoot open. "Uh . . . to fish?"

He grins at me. "Someone's had her head underground for a while now," he says. "She hasn't even kept an eye on her astronomy news."

"Why, is there a comet tonight?" I do a quick scan of the skies for anything unusual.

He smiles again, finishes the rest of his beer, and tosses the empty bottle into a plastic bag. "I've never known my *linda* to forget a single lunar eclipse since she was . . ." He brings his hands close together to indicate a little baby Chloé.

"The eclipse is tonight?" My eyes go wide. I can't believe it totally slipped my mind.

"*Ese* Gordon is taking up a lot of your brain cells. Just make sure you leave some for other things. He's a nice kid, but at this age, even nice kids have their own hormones in mind."

"He's not like that, Papi."

"They're *all* like that, *linda*," he fires back. He wants me to get this and get it good. "*I* was like that, and I think I'm a pretty nice guy. So be careful."

"Okay, I got it." A wave rocks the boat to a nice little peak, then lulls again. My dad pops open another beer, then lies back to watch the moon. I know he's done with his lecture, if you can even call it that, but I'm left wondering if he's right. If all guys are like that, then why don't I feel like Gordon is taking advantage of me?

For a good twenty minutes, we say nothing, just watch the sky and wait. Then, little by little, the lower edge of the moon starts to flatten out, a dark penumbral shadow replacing its curve. It's amazing to think that's us—our giant, massive planet—getting in the way of the sun's light.

I try to imagine my dad as a teenager before he met my mom. How many girlfriends did he have? Did he love any of them? How did he feel about adopting me? Thinking about him from different angles makes me feel in tune with him, yet disconnected at the same time. I'll never completely know him and his secrets. And in a strange daughterly way, I don't really want to.

I glance over to see if he's still awake, appreciating the heavenly show. His eyes are slits, but open. Out of his peripheral vision, he catches me watching him and flashes one of his cute Papi smiles. An *adorable* Papi smile. I smile back. The creeping shadow finally stretches across the moon's surface, covering it with an intense shade of reddish orange, and I can't help but think that my dad is a bit like a lunar eclipse—obscure in his umbral shadows but still visible, still beautiful, and still there when I look for him.

Spring break finally arrives, and I could not be more elated to sleep the mornings away. For a whole week, I will not have to see ancient Rooney or deal with any equations. I help my mom out with the babies during the day, and discover that a mom with help is a Happy Mom. Some mornings, I find Rock asleep on my front porch, at which point he comes in for breakfast, watches old VH-1 reruns with my mom, then leaves like he's on a mission. I don't ask where anymore.

On Wednesday morning, I wake to the sound of the house phone ringing, my mother laughing, then her footsteps inside the babies' room. I don't remember much else, because I doze off again, dreaming of a warm, sandy beach and the faraway smell of grilled ham and cheese.

"Chloé, come eat!" I hear someone calling me from down the beach.

A deep hunger shoots through me, sending me the urgent

message to wake up and get my butt over to a kitchen-counter stool. As if I haven't seen food for days. "Yay, breakfast," I mumble, rubbing my eyes.

"It's noon. I take it you're enjoying your time off?" Mom says, sliding a sandwich onto a plate and cutting it in half. In no more than four seconds, I have eaten through the first half.

"Yep."

"Rock called a little while ago."

"Why didn't he call my phone?"

"I don't know. He called to see if you were home. He probably didn't want to wake you."

"What did he say?"

"That he'll be home today if you need him and that he's been bothering us too much. He apologized for 'loitering like a leech.'" She laughs, shakes her head. "He's not a bother to anyone, poor thing."

"He could've just called me and told me that."

"Maybe he wanted someone else to talk to. You've been spending so much time with Gordon, honey. I think maybe he's just feeling a little . . . I don't know . . . rejected, maybe?"

I nod, finishing off the rest of the sandwich with a wad of guilt in my throat. I'll talk to him later. "Can I have another one?"

"Sure." She starts on another sandwich, then says, "You know, I feel bad for Rock sometimes. We're like his family." She looks at me for a quick second, then goes back to fiddling in the kitchen. "It's sad. It makes me appreciate that my mom and dad were around to raise us, as much as I complain about them."

I nod. Is this her way of telling me I shouldn't go seeking answers about my adoption case? Because if it is . . . *sigh*. "Yes, and we should appreciate whoever loves us whether our DNA matches or not. I get it."

She stops and looks at me. "That's not what I was going to say." Our eyes connect, and I can just barely see my uncle's expression in hers for a quick second. She serves up another sandwich, cuts it in half, then slides it over to me. "What I was going to say is that I took my dad for granted, but had he not been a part of my life, I would've wanted to know him. So if you want help finding your birth parents, Chloé . . ."—the spatula in her hand trembles slightly— "it's okay. I'll help you."

I look down at my ham and cheese, melted American oozing out of the sides, sticking to the plate. Suddenly, I'm not so hungry anymore. I appreciate that, but I'd feel better doing it alone. "Okay," I say.

I force the sandwich down, thank my mom for lunch, then trudge back to my room.

Every time Rock has called today, he has made it a point to tell me that he is not doing anything, just watching TV in his room all day. This is an attempt, I fear, to prove that he is capable of abstinence and that I am wrong about him. As a result, I have to constantly switch lines while on the phone with Gordon to talk to Rock when he calls.

"It's Rock again," I mumble into the phone.

"Tell him you're feeding your brothers or something."

"I can't. He's in a depressive state."

"I've noticed. I *have* tried to tell you."

"I—I know, Gordon. But it's weird. I can't stop being his friend either. It would kill him."

"But you can't be his therapist either. He's too emotionally connected to you."

"But I am," I say, realizing I'm being totally honest here. "And he's my therapist too. I'm sorry, I know he's a guy, but that's just how it is."

"So . . ." He's quiet for a few seconds. He clears his throat. "You tell him about us? About private stuff?"

"Normally I would, but things have changed. I have to wait until he has a new girlfriend before I can tell him anything so he doesn't feel sorry for himself. Right now, he thinks he's in love with me."

"I could have told you that the first time I met him," he says. I stare at my ceiling fan, absorbing the echo of Gordon's words. So it's apparent to others, not just me.

"He's not in love with me, Gordon. He's just . . . needy. He needs someone at all times."

I don't tell him that I think maybe Rock's profession of love is real this time. That maybe all those other times were real too, they were just leading up to this one. Rock has never abstained for a whole week since he lost his virginity four years ago. Since then, it's been wall-to-wall women.

"Are you doing anything right now?" I ask.

"I guess I could take a break now. Why?"

"Can we meet at the dock? I'm dying to see you."

I've been going crazy thinking about our times alone in his room all this week, times that are slowly leading up to the inevitable . . . for which I now feel I'm ready. All week, he's been very sweet and he lets go of his authoritative personality when we're together. I love the look on his face when he realizes that girls rule and that I hold power of my own, therefore he can't possibly know all the answers of the universe.

"I'm leaving now," he says, and I'm out the door four seconds later.

It's time Gordon learned another one of the dock's secrets. The estuary is great for swimming. There's no slimy surface today. The water is clear, down to the bottom. There's fish all around, but so what? It's ninety degrees outside. Cooling off is the only option.

I pull off my shorts, leaving on my underwear and bra as swim gear, and jump, cannonball style. "Weeeee!" I squeal, crashing into the water's surface, the bubbly silence surrounding me in the warm water. When I come up, I see Gordon standing at the dock's edge, hands on his hips.

"I can't believe you just did that. That water is nasty. What if there are gators in there?"

"Then we'll get eaten. Jump in, babe. Or are you chicken?"

He tilts his head to one side, like he's debating whether or not to accept the challenge.

"*Bock, bock, bock* . . . chicken!" I taunt, splashing water up at him.

Determined to prove that he is not, in fact, poultry, Gordon pulls off his T-shirt and jumps in. A bigger splash could not be possible. The waves he creates are tsunami-sized. I swallow a small amount of lightly salted water.

He comes up for air, hair plastered to his forehead. "How's that for chicken?"

"Whoa, you really showed me." I paddle up to him and boldly wrap my legs around his waist.

Instinctively, he grabs hold of me. "You shouldn't do that."

"And why not?"

He chews on his lower lip. "It's dangerous."

"What is this obsession of yours with danger?" I kiss him. In the background, I hear my phone ringing. Rock must be breaking down and needs me before he falls off the abstinence wagon. But I can't talk to him right now. He's going to have to deal with things without me.

"It's addictive." Gordon kisses me back.

I don't know if it's the sun, the water amplifying things, or what, but this is it. Something of sexual significance will definitely happen today. Gordon is definitely the one.

I reach behind my back to unclasp my bra. It's water-logged anyway.

"What are you doing?" he asks, breaking the kiss.

"Being dangerous." I hurl my bra onto the dock.

He smiles big. "You're crazy, you know that? What if someone sees you?" His eyes glance down quickly.

"Nobody's coming. Your turn, chicken. *Bock, bock, bock.*" I tug on his shorts. I bet he won't do it.

But because he loves to prove me wrong, he makes a face like I'm a loser and pulls off his shorts. Not just his shorts, but everything! He whirls them around, imitating me, and flings them onto the dock. They land near my bra with a huge, wet thud.

I laugh the loudest I have laughed in a while. "I can't believe you did that!"

"Thank God, I thought you were laughing at something else." He pulls me back onto him, wrapping my legs around his waist again. There's only one piece of clothing left between us, and believe me, it's not much. Thoughts flood my mind. What if I get pregnant? Is that what happened to my birth mother?

"What's wrong?" His concerned look snaps me out of my reverie.

"If I take this last thing off . . ." I can hear the nerves in my voice. "What's going to happen? Will it be a mistake?"

He touches his forehead to mine. "That's up to you. But I don't see how it could be, Chloé. I love you." He blinks softly, his lashes stuck together. His face is so beautiful right now.

"I love you too," I say. And I know then that if anything terrible or unexpected were to happen, I would be able to handle it. We would handle it together. We kiss again.

Next thing I know, I am taking off my panties, without the slightest bit of regret. I ball them up and throw them onto the dock, taking in everything about our surroundings—the sun, the sky, the sound of fish slapping nearby. I feel confident knowing this is about to happen in my perfect place with my perfect guy.

Gordon holds me tight and kisses my cheek. I can tell he wants to show me that there's no rush, that I'm in control of this situation.

Suddenly, I hear it. A rumbling engine coming up the road. Not the survey guys. Not a lost vehicle. But a '68 Mustang driven by the only other person to have ever shared this special place with me. A person naïve enough to think he's still alone in that honor.

Sputtering turbo sounds grow closer.

Gordon follows my gaze. "Someone's here."

"Rock," I tell him.

He lets go of me and starts swimming toward the dock. "What are you going to tell him?"

"I have no freakin' clue." Even though Rock knows that Gordon and I are alone a lot, seeing us here will definitely induce a wake-up call. There's no time to even climb onto the dock for our clothes.

I see the black hood of the Mustang slide up, crunching over the gravel. I hope he has enough decency to leave when he sees that my bike and Gordon's car are here together.

"Go away, Rock," I mumble.

The Mustang lingers, the sound of her engine filling the estuary. Gordon watches me from under the dock. I paddle toward him, but not so close that I can't see what's happening onshore. My phone rings, but it stops after two seconds, like Rock realized it was a bad idea to call. I hear the Mustang change gears, then it turns around in the gravel and heads back down the road again.

I exhale loudly.

"Chloé, you'd better go talk to him," Gordon says, pulling himself up onto the dock. I look away, embarrassed. It's one thing to see someone lying next to you naked, and another to see them climbing out of water that way.

He reaches down to help me up, handing me my clothes as I land on the wooden planks. "I don't need to. He's not a baby. Stay, Gordon. Don't let him scare you off."

Gordon pulls on his wet shorts and lies flat on his

back. "No. You need to talk to him," he repeats, and I know our special moment is over for now. He's right. Rock's probably wounded. He didn't expect this, and I need to have an honest talk with him. But couldn't it wait another hour?

"Fine," I say, disappointed that our afternoon dissolved into this. Maybe the universe is trying to tell me something. Maybe today wasn't the day. I hate signs and I hate warnings, so it's no surprise that I get dressed quickly and jump on Lolita to leave. "I'll call you later."

"Chloé," Gordon says.

"Yes?" I hate feeling like he's using this opportunity to stop and think about what we almost did together. I don't feel any regret, and neither should he.

"Don't be mad. We had a great afternoon together." He smiles.

I nod in response.

I remember those first times in tutoring. How hard it was to get him to loosen up. Yet today, he jumped right into the estuary and peeled off his shorts. Isn't that what I wanted? For him to put the world on hold and just have fun? Still, I can't shake the irrational, gnawing feeling that he's trying to get rid of me.

"I shouldn't have met you now anyway," he says, and I almost can't believe what I'm hearing. "I was up to my ears in work."

I don't respond, just wait until he closes his car door, has gone down the driveway, and turned onto the main road. Then I put my head down on Lolita and take in the sudden stillness of the swamp.

Twenty-one

Rock sits on my bedroom floor, running his pocketknife underneath his grimy nails. In my girly yellow room, he looks about as comfortable as a cat in a bathtub. Per my father's instructions a few years back, Rock is not allowed to sit on my bed under any circumstances—a pretty dumb rule if you think about it. If we were going to have sex, we could still do it on the floor.

"Are you going to say anything?" I ask, sitting cross-legged on my bed.

"You're the one who called me here."

"I know, but . . ."

"How long have you guys been going there, Chloé?" He

looks up, the angle of his jaw sharp. The way he says "Chloé" makes my heart hurt a little.

"Since we've been seeing each other, Rock. He's my boyfriend. What'd you expect?"

"If you didn't think it was a big deal, then why haven't you mentioned it?" He shoots me a hard stare.

"Because I know hearing about us together bothers you. I guess that's why you've kept your distance, but I really would like for us to all be friends."

"Look, you don't have to explain anything to me. It's your life, your decisions." His tanned arms look strong over his knees as he slides the sharp point of the knife underneath each nail. "Chloé, you have every right to be with whoever you want, but that doesn't mean I have to pretend I'm okay with it, so don't worry about me anymore."

"I do worry about you. I worry that you're not sleeping at home, that you're going to catch a disease . . ." I watch him cleaning his nails. "That you're putting that dirt on my floor." Hopefully, he'll laugh. I miss hearing him laugh.

He smiles faintly.

"The dock won't be there much longer anyway. They're kicking me out."

He raises an eyebrow, looks up at me with heavy lids.

"They're going to build something there, can you believe it?"

"When did that happen?"

"Back in January."

"Back in January, and now's when you tell me? See, this is what I'm talking about, sweetheart. No communication anymore. Where's the love?" He flips his hands up in exasperation.

"Well, Rock, you've been coming and going a lot lately. And I know what evils you're up to when you're missing in action."

"What? I've been calling you all day, Chloé!" he answers with the same accusing tone.

"Today, yes, but what about the other days?"

"The other days, I'm trying to drown out a crappy existence," he says, all serious.

I just stare at him. I don't know if he means that, or if this is Rock playing the "save me" role again. "You don't mean that."

"No, of course I don't," he says, going back to picking the last of his nails.

I sigh. "Rock, the point is, I have to say good-bye to the dock, and I want you there when I do. Not Gordon." Hopefully, bestowing him with that honor will remind him I love him.

"Gee, thanks."

"You know, you're being a big baby. You could be a little more understanding."

"Waaah." He closes and reopens his pocketknife over and over. "They can't make you leave."

"Uh, yes, they can. I don't own that land."

"*Agh, pfft,*" he grunts, biting the tiny corner of a nail and spitting it out.

"It's *our* place," I say. And it is. I love Gordon, but he's still just a visitor. "We'll need to hang out there every day, you and me, and say good-bye."

"Our place," he repeats, lost in thought.

His face—his eyes—are killing me. Is it possible to love two people at the same time? I know Rock thought we'd have something together, and maybe if neither of us ever ends up with anyone else it could work—you know, for the sake of procreation and not being lonely—but right now, I'm in love with someone who's pretty great. And I have to tell Rock that. "There's something else."

He looks at me cautiously.

"But you have to promise not to get mad, or else I'll have trouble telling you anything ever again, and then I'll know for sure we can no longer be friends."

"You're banging that dude."

My brain flashes a lovely image of me and Gordon together, skin touching skin, arms and legs twisted together. "Not yet, but—"

"That looks says it all." He lies flat on my floor and stretches his arms. "I know you are, doll. You don't have to rub it in my face."

"I'm not rubbing anything."

"Yeah, you are."

"Stop it, Rock." From my position on the bed, I pick up my pillow and chuck it at him. "We haven't done it yet. But I want to."

He hugs the pillow and shakes his head, a sad smile on his lips. "Don't you realize I know these things, Chlo? I know them before you even tell me."

"I still wanted you to hear it from me."

"Yeah? Well, thanks, but I kind of figured it out when I saw his car and your bike there together. And because we *are* friends, I should be able to tell you if I think you're making a big mistake, so guess what? I think you're making a big mistake."

"You're not making this any better. I know you think I should be with you, but get over it. Friends who hook up can't go back to the place they were before. And I don't want to lose you!" Why am I yelling?

Rock sits up straight, an incredulous look on his face. "How do you know that? How do you know that we're not meant to be together, like your parents? I spend my life here because of them and you. I want my kids to have a family like that."

"But it doesn't happen like that for everyone. They're freaks," I fire back.

"How will we know if we don't even try?" He yells back so loudly, I almost start crying. He sees the pain on my face and quickly regains his composure. *Jesus*. I run my hands through my hair.

"Gordon is really sweet," I say slowly, registering the look of contempt on his face before continuing. "You haven't bothered to get to know him."

He throws his hands up. "What the hell do you want from me, Chloé?"

"You can start by being happy for me!" I yell.

"Fine!" he yells back. "I'm happy for you!"

"Augh!" I feel like worlds are colliding inside my chest. I can't handle this anymore. "Just go home. I have to study."

"You have to study? *Pfft*. You're already becoming him."

"Oh, what. I can't study now? That has nothing to do with Gordon."

"Stop saying that retard's name."

"Stop calling him a retard," I snap.

"Whatever." He settles into a fake restful position.

I sigh. "If I fail that class, my parents take away Lolita. And if they take away the bike, I lose my soul, Rock, okay? I thought if anyone could understand that, it'd be you."

He closes his eyes.

If he wants to be an ass about this, that's his choice.

"You know what the worst part about this is?" I ask, meeting his stubborn eyes with my own. "Week after week, you assume I'll just accept the girls you hook up with—most of them I've never even seen, never even known their names. And now I ask you to accept one guy—*one* guy—and you won't. I'm happy for the first time since Seth died and you can't be happy for me. Well, I'm not going to let you spoil this." I get up and open the door to my room.

"I'm sorry, Chlo. I just can't," he says as I charge out.

"Oh, grow the fuck up," I say over my shoulder.

He can follow me if he wants to, or he can fall asleep in my room for all I care. I'm going out. I snatch Lolita's key off the hook in the kitchen, but my mother comes out of the pantry, one baby in a front sling, one baby on a back sling. "Where you going?"

"Out." I grab my helmet off the counter and head for the garage.

"Stop," my mom says. The baby in the front carrier turns his head toward me like he's going to lecture me too.

I stare at her. "Stop what?"

"You're not going anywhere."

"I always go out after dinner." It's not like my mother to stop me, especially these days. I need my space.

"Sit down, Chloé." Her bright hair hangs in loose curls around her face. The circles under her eyes are getting lighter. Babies sleeping more equals Mommy regaining strength.

I lean against the counter. Whatever she wants to tell me, she can tell me as I stand. "What is it, Mom?"

"Marraine tells me you've been leaving school with Gordon. Is that true?"

My gut clenches. "No," I lie. "I only left one day during second period. The other days were during lunch. I went to get something to eat."

"Leaving school during lunch isn't allowed."

"I—" I thought she didn't know about that new rule. And I certainly didn't think Marraine had seen me leaving. She always takes lunch in the teachers' lounge.

"She says you failed your last two chemistry tests, Chloé." She waits, her eyes wistful, her mouth a thin line.

"How would she know that? *I* don't even know what I got on the last one."

"You got an F."

"What?"

"She works at your school, Chloé. Stop acting so gullible!" Her voice raises right at the end. Frustrated, she closes her eyes and relaxes, stroking Baby Sagan's head to calm herself down.

"She's making that up, Mom! That's not true." Behind me, I hear the front door close gently as Rock makes his stealthy exit. I'm sure this is all very amusing to him.

My mother shakes her head, because we both know

Marraine has no reason to lie. "Chloé," she says slowly, "I know you're perfectly capable of making good decisions when you put your mind to it, but right now, honey, you're not considering the consequences of what you're doing."

"And what is that, Mom? What exactly am I doing?"

Her calm little smile tells me she knows. She's not stupid. After all, my mother used to skip school all the time to be with my father. "You need a new tutor, so I'm going to hire one for you."

"No. I have Gordon."

"Gordon," she stresses, "is not helping you anymore in that respect. He has no problem leaving campus with you. If he had any regard for you or your failing grade, he'd stay in school all day and urge you to do the same."

"You can't talk, Mom. You had a boyfriend who skipped with you too. So you can't tell me anything."

"I most certainly did not."

"You most certainly did too. Sethie told me."

The look of shock on her face is superb. *Ha! So there!*

"Seth was only ten. He wouldn't have known anything. Besides, he was always in school when I'd come home with—"

I smile. "When you came home with . . . who?"

She doesn't answer, just presses her lips together in frustration.

I lower my voice and try to sound adult about this, in the hope that she'll treat me like one. "When I said I would bring up the grade, I meant it. You have to believe me."

"I don't have to anything. Chloé, you have a D average. Do you hear me? A D average. Now, I know that Mr.

Rooney is not the best teacher, and I know that chemistry has never been your strong suit, but a deal is a deal, and when your father gets home tonight, he's going to hear about this."

"Mom! Please! I'll pull up the grade. I've hit a roadblock, but I'll get back on track, I swear!"

"Chloé, leave the key and go back to your room."

"No!"

I can't. My eyes well up, but I can't bring myself to leave the key. She can't do this to me. She should understand! I make a mental note to never be such a bitch to my daughter if I ever have one, adopted or not.

"Excuse me?" she says. And for the first time in a year, I see my mother again—the one who participated in my life before the babies were born. Her eyebrows draw together, her lips form a tight knot, her teeth grind hard.

"Mom . . ."

"Leave the key on the counter and go back to your room." She says this gently, like it's any easier that way. "Nobody's asking you to love school, Chloé, but I can't have you running around, failing chemistry, skipping class, getting yourself hurt."

"Who says I'm getting hurt? Now you sound like Rock!" I'm always careful the way I talk to her, but right now, I don't care. She doesn't understand. She doesn't understand what she's doing to me.

"And that's why I've always loved that boy."

Like that's supposed to be funny. *Ha, ha! Ha, ha . . . not.* It's one thing for Rock to sing his own praises, but now my mother? Enough already.

I face her and cross my arms. "Since when do you care what I do with my life? I go out every night without a problem, and *now* is when you care?" I feel like I'm spitting venom, but if she's going to take away Lolita, then I've got nothing to lose at this point. "You're the one always calling me a wanderer, saying I'm destined to roam the Earth! You're the one always comparing me to Seth!"

A comparison I now wholly cherish.

"You don't know what you're talking about. I have *always* cared about you, more than anybody. I know you adored Seth, baby, but listen to me: Seth had nothing. Whatever he did have, he gave it up."

"What do you mean?"

She shakes her head. "His job, his future . . . the bike, Chloé. That's all he had, and he gave it to you. Is that how you want to end up? With a motorcycle and little else? We're trying to help you. What are your goals? What do you want from this life?"

How dare she? As if her life goal was to marry Papi, work at the Pancake House, and get pregnant at the age of thirty-seven by surprise, with twins, no less! Who is she to demand anything from me? Who cares how I choose to live my life, as long as I'm good to people and don't hurt anyone?

I am sick of this. Why should I keep explaining myself to others? "Nothing. I want nothing," I say, slamming the key down on the kitchen counter, my chest aching as I do.

I burst out of the kitchen and head for the front door. She may take Lolita away, but that won't stop me from leaving the house. I expect some resistance, but it seems my mother has used up her reserves. She lets me go without another word.

And I do go. And go. And go. It takes me an hour in the cool night, but I walk three miles, all the way to the Murphys' dock.

Twenty-two

Y ou can depend on the night sky. You can count on the constellations. While some stars do burn out eventually, it'll be light-years before anyone ever sees that happen. Even when the sun is down and clouds cover Earth, the night sky is there.

I need the stars.

Constant.

Dependable.

Orderly.

I try calling Gordon so he can come pick me up, but he doesn't answer. Considering what nearly transpired this afternoon, not to mention the fact that I defended the crap out of him against Rock, the *least* he could do is answer the freakin' phone. *Sorry, Chloé, I have to study*, he could say, and that'd be it. I'd understand.

I call Rock next and at least he picks up. "Heard you getting burned by your mom," he says, his voice smooth and deep.

"Whatever." A faint light streaks across the sky, but I don't wish for anything. Wishes are bullshit.

"You need to figure out what you want, little girl," he says, all sagelike.

"Listen," I grunt, "if I wanted to get another earful, I would've stayed home with my mom. You're supposed to be my shoulder to lean on. I should be able to tell you anything without you judging me. You're the only one I can count on."

"I'm glad you're finally starting to see that."

"You suck. Good-bye."

"Relax, I get it," he says. "Yes, I'll always be here for you if you need me. Always."

I smile and close my eyes. Rock Nuñez, a luminous supergiant in the Andromeda Galaxy. There, anytime I need him.

The frogs sing me a soft tune. I should add frogs to my list of dependable things. *Thank you, little* ranitas. "Sorry for everything," I mumble.

"It's okay. I'm the one who's sorry. For a lot of things, Chloé. For acting like a dick today. And for slamming on the Russian dude. I promise, I won't bother you about it anymore."

"You were just looking out for me. I know." I cut him off before he can say anything else.

"Anyway . . ." He draws the word out slowly, and I catch

dead air on the line right at the end. Another call. "I gotta go. That's Amber."

"What the hell, Rock?"

"Her and Vince, calling it quits. That's why I kept calling you today."

"Jesus." The air turns sweet. Gray clouds slowly move over the night like a curtain closing down a show.

"Later, doll."

"Later."

Great. Amber's back. And now the vicious cycle will begin again. She'll fuck with his head and he'll turn to booty calls. Maybe he's right. Maybe I *am* the only one who can save him. But what would I get out of the deal? *Probably an STD*, I hear Sethie say, and my laughter is carried out to space by the breeze.

In the stillness of my room, my phone plays Gordon's assigned tune. But only for a moment. I check my phone. MISSED CALL—BRAIN BOY—12:26 A.M. Do I call back? Yes. I call and wait, my heart jittering me. I watch the Harley Santa alarm clock's red glow in the darkness. Outside, a light rain hits my window.

He answers. "Hey."

"Hey, what's up?"

"Nothing."

"You just called me," I remind him.

"I know."

"Were you afraid I'd be sleeping?"

"Yeah." He sounds unsure. I'm not crazy about the way his voice wavers.

"Are you okay? You sound weird."

"I'm fine. I just saw that you called earlier."

"Oh. Okay." *God, Gordon, is that all?* I was hoping for an *I love you,* just to confirm we're still good. "You're fine, except for the whole thing with Rock showing up, right?"

"Yeah, that was weird."

"Yeah." A strange silence settles between us.

"Chloé, I have to be honest with you about something."

"Okay." My heart leaps into my throat. "What is it?"

"My parents have been on my case the last few weeks. They know I'm seeing someone, and they're not down with the whole idea of my spending so much time away from stuff that needs doing."

I release a breath I didn't even know I was holding. "It's okay, Gordon. My mom's on my case too. She knows about me skipping school with you. And my chem grade hasn't gotten any better, which doesn't help."

"She knows? That's my fault, Chloé. This is another problem."

"There's no problem," I say quickly before he goes and thinks we're making a big mistake by being together. "We just have to make a point to study harder and take breaks from each other. Let's do that over the weekend and then see each other at school on Monday, okay? We'll take it from there." God, that is really hard to say when all I want is to be alone with him again, but we need to go about this the right way. We have to prove to our parents that we can handle a relationship along with school.

Suddenly, though, his voice sounds different. Cold. "Sounds great. See you Monday. Thank you."

Sounds great? Thank you? His mom must be around. I wait on the line.

"Chloé?" he whispers after a minute.

"Yeah?" I hate feeling like a secret, yet I can't seem to say anything else.

"Look, I can't talk right now. The walls have ears. But I love you. We'll talk tomorrow."

Whew.

I might've lost Lolita tonight, but that's the only thing I'll be losing. Gordon and I are just going through a glitch here. There was bound to be one after two and a half months.

"Okay." I let the disappointment in my voice travel through the ether, across the distance, into Gordon's *humongonoid* mansion in Palmetto Heights, right into his anal but lovely brain. "I love you too."

Monday, it's back to school. Rock is at my house bright and early, asleep on my porch swing when I come outside. I nudge his head with my boot.

"We still racing?" he mumbles.

"In the Durango?" I ask, looking at the old, gray elephant I'm lucky enough to take to school today now that Lolita is off-limits.

"I could just take you."

"No, I have tutoring after school."

"So then why doesn't Gordon just bring you home afterward?"

"'Cause . . ." I hesitate. "My mom has a problem with him now."

I see his eyebrows go up as he makes a face. "Me, I'm not gonna say nothin'. Nothin' at all."

"Good. Let's just go, shall we?"

I try racing Rock in the truck, but he blows past so fast, I am nearly swallowed by the Mustang's wake. SUVs suck *huevos*.

At school, I go all six periods without seeing Gordon. That's four days now, with only a few checkup calls, nothing emotional. And after the way he sounded the other day, it's starting to freak me out. I know he had some tests today, so he's probably off studying somewhere. At worst, I'll see him at peer tutoring.

During trig, the last period of the day, I can hardly stand it anymore. I have to see him. I have to sink into his hug, touch his dimples, and know that everything is still okay between us. My stomach swirls around, all turbulent and panicky.

One minute until the bell.

My mind is already sprinting down the hall, dodging people on my way to the auditorium, and when the bell finally rings, I'm out of the gate, running to win the Triple Crown.

I catch glimpses of people—Vincent hollering annoyingly down the hall, Amber and a friend, deep in discussion in a corner—but I can't slow down. I'm on a mission to get to peer tutoring. When I reach the auditorium, all out of breath, I stop to regroup just outside the door. I pretend to be on a very important phone call, just in case Sabine is watching, so she doesn't think anything is wrong.

As I wait, I notice it's going to rain yet again. Of course it is, it's April in South Florida.

Gordon should be here by now. Could he already be inside? He might've taken his last test and come in early, and that's why I haven't seen him. A smile ready at my lips, I pull open the noisy auditorium doors.

I do a quick visual scan of the rows and rows of seats. The usual people are there, although there are a few newcomers as well, now that the last grading period is well under way. Ms. Rath waves a hello to me from the stage. I give her a little wave back. Sabine eyes me like a jealous salamander from her throne of paper clips.

All is as usual. But no Gordon. He's late.

To pass the time I read a chapter in my book, but all I can really think about is our skinny-dipping at the dock, kissing in the water . . . It felt so right to be that close to him. If he felt the same way, wouldn't he brave his parents and bring me further into his life? *Where are you, Gordon?*

I feel someone standing next to me and look up. Gene Simmons is crouching next to me in a flowered dress. "Chloé."

"Oh, hey, Ms. Rath."

"Gordon should be on his way. I know he was in school today."

"He was?" I do nothing to hide my surprise. My pen *tap-tap-taps* my notebook. "Thanks," I say, hoping she'll leave me alone to my anxiety attack. What's going on? Did the weekend break give him too much time to think?

I try calling him, but his phone goes to voice mail. "Hey,

sweetie. I'm here, waiting for you. Hurry up, I don't think my heart can take it any longer."

Half an hour later, I'm still sitting here, stood up by my so-called boyfriend. Sabine glances over at me every so often with a look I perceive as victorious. *Happy?* I give her a minimal smile as I quietly get up to head for the door. Only when I've blown past the noisy doors and charged into the parking lot do I let out a piercing shriek. But since it's raining gutter-gushing torrents, no one's around to hear me.

Twenty-three

Inside the Durango I call Gordon one more time. If he doesn't answer, then I'm calling his house. Screw his parents. I have to talk to him. If there's a problem between us, we can work it out.

He answers on the third ring this time. "Hey, Chloé."

"Oh, hey! Where've you been all day?" I try to keep my voice light.

"I've had a crazy day, you have no idea."

"Yeah, I'll bet. But . . . did you forget about tutoring?"

"I'm sorry about that, but I cannot discuss it right now."

"What? Why *cannot* you discuss it, Gordon? *Do* you *not* have one minute to explain what's going on?" I know I sound like a smart-ass, but I deserve an explanation.

"Hold on . . ." he says, sounding like he's going somewhere quiet to talk. I'm right. When he comes back on the line, his voice is quieter but clearer. "Chloé, please don't take this the wrong way, but . . . I need a few days. There's a lot going on at home. My parents have really been coming down on me. I don't have the perpetual freedom you have at your house, okay?"

"You make it sound like I have no rules just because my parents aren't as strict as yours. But if they don't like us being together so much, then fine. We'll cut down some."

"That's not it, Chloé. You don't understand. They . . ." He hesitates. I don't like the way this is sounding. "They don't even know about you. It's not that I'm not allowed to have a girlfriend, but let's just say it's not encouraged."

"You told me they knew you were seeing someone."

"Someone, yes. I haven't told them exactly who."

"What's wrong with who you're seeing?" I can't believe I'm hearing this. "So you mean I've been your dirty little secret this whole time? Can't you just introduce me? What is the big, hairy deal? I'm not a heathen, you know. Don't give in to their prejudices, Gordon."

"I'm not, but you're being . . . You're being linear again, Chloé. It's not that simple."

"Nothing is simple, Rock, I know that!" My voice reverberates inside the truck.

Silence. "Did you . . . just call me Rock?"

What? "I mean, Gordon. Sorry." God, *what* is wrong with me? "Look, I just . . . wish you'd had enough consideration to call me and explain things, instead of hiding like a freakin' coward." I try controlling my voice but end up yelling those last few words.

"Can you express yourself without screaming like a banshee? I can understand you just fine without your tone."

"Go to hell," I tell him. How's that for tone? I have a right to be mad. I didn't like his condescending way of talking to me when we first met, and I sure as shit don't like it now. What kind of guy can't stand up to his parents for what he believes in, for a person he *loves*? Suddenly, I realize this isn't helping. I close my eyes and refocus my energies. "Sorry," I mumble.

He sighs. "No, I'm sorry. You're right, I should have called you. But just . . . do your own thing for a few days so my parents can get off my back. Then we'll take it from there, okay?"

Is this the beginning of the end? 'Cause that's what this feels like.

"Yeah, Gordon. That's just fine. We'll take a break from each other." And as stupid and dramatic as it is, I hang up on him. I know I probably just knocked our chances of getting through this back a couple of notches, but as my mother would say, the moon is in retrograde tonight, and when that happens, Chloe's irreversible.

I can't go to the dock because it's raining, and I can't go home because that would make my mom feel like she won some battle in taking away Lolita. I will *not* go to Gordon's house, because I have some dignity. So I head off in search of the only person who can make me feel better when the planets are not lining up. Rock.

I'm sure he'll be thrilled to hear this.

The Durango's wipers swish urgently, but not fast enough to clear the amount of water on the windshield. My lashes are not doing an efficient enough job of clearing the tears from my eyes, either. To make matters worse, I feel so defeated driving this truck. I promised Seth I would take care of Lolita, but I haven't even been able to do that. Now she's locked up in the garage. *I've let you down, Sethie. I've let myself down too.*

I remember when Seth sat in this very seat next to me, teaching me to drive when I was barely twelve. He told me I was a natural, like I'd been driving my whole life. And in a way, I had been. To this day, I have always been happiest when behind the wheel of some car or truck, or behind the handlebars of Lolita—in control of something. Gordon was right about one thing. I am Motor Girl.

When I turn onto Rock's street, I expect to see a new car in his driveway. But his Mustang's there alone. Thank God.

Jumping out of the truck in the slamming rain, I shut the door hard and nearly wipe out on the slick grass trying to get to his front door. Under the shelter of the front step overhang, I tap on the door screen.

"Hello?" I try the door handle and the door creaks open.

I close it softly behind me and step into the dark living room. The blinds are all tightly shut, the same old sofas from when we were little sit unused and full of dust. The faint smell of his dad's cigarette smoke lingers in the air. Rock's TV is on loud.

"Hello?" I call out again, creeping closer to the short

hallway that leads to the three bedrooms, inching around boxes of stored stuff that never made it out to the garage. Rock's room is at the back of the house. I step over a cardboard tube that's blocking my way like a fallen tree in the woods. From here, I can hear the voices on the TV, and through his half-open door, I see Rock's back without a shirt on, sculptured and tanned. His jeans are on, then I can't see anything else because he moves away. I feel stupid standing here. It's been so long since I set foot into this house and it's just not the same place it used to be. Maybe I headed over here a little too blindly.

Why am I creeping around?

I'm *this* close to calling out his name again, when another figure comes into view. It's someone bending over to pull down what's left of her attire, a girl standing there naked, shaking out her hair. Brunette with blond highlights.

I step back, but the cardboard tube trips me, sending me tumbling backward as I try to regain my balance. I use the wall as a springboard and bolt for the door before Rock has the chance to catch me, though I hear him calling, "Hold on!" from the hallway.

I stumble out of the house and into the rain, but I'm still fumbling for the key, which I'd shoved into my pocket, when Rock appears at the door. "Chloé, what are you doing here?"

All I can do is stand there getting wet while I try to find my key, but it's not in my pocket after all. "I came to talk to you."

"Are you okay?"

"Just dandy." I find the key lying in the grass. I pick it up and jam it into the lock.

"It's Gordon, isn't it?"

"It's nothing. Good-bye."

"You don't have to go, Chloé."

I give him a hard look. "I think I do. You're busy."

He closes the door quietly. "I'll take her home."

"No. Don't do that. Just . . . just . . ." I don't know why I'm so flustered. I know all about Rock's wanton lifestyle, so this shouldn't have come as a surprise to me.

His eyebrows twist in confusion, he waits to hear anything I might have to say, but my words are stuck as the rain soaks through my jeans. This is the worst fucking day ever. Strike that. The second worst.

I finally wrench the truck door open, and I jump in, turning on the ignition. "Chloeeee," he tries cheering me up, but his voice can't work its usual magic today. "Come on, baby," he whines.

"Rock!" I snap. "I'm not going to stay here and wait for your 'guest,' or should I say *customer*, to leave. I have no business here anyway."

"You have *every* business here," he says firmly.

"No. We're nothing! You and I are nothing!" I hiss, even though we are definitely something, and I feel I have the right to demand that little slut leave his house.

"And whose fault is that?" He tries raising his voice at me, but it's controlled. Even when he's losing patience with me.

"Yours!" I shout. "Maybe if you weren't whoring around all the time, I might let myself get close to you. But you said you'd stop, and look—you can't."

"You gave me the red light, Chloé. You made it perfectly clear nothing would ever happen between us."

"Yes, because I can't compete. Okay? I just can't," I say. "How can I trust that someone better isn't going to come along, Rock? Someone prettier, with a better body. I'm afraid. Don't you get it . . . afraid?"

His look is priceless. "What are you talking about, Chlo? I didn't know you felt that way. You're always saying you don't want to lose me as a friend, so that's all I thought this was about."

"It *is* Rock, but come on . . . don't you think I would love for it to work out between us? Obviously, I would. But one: Chances are it won't. And two . . ." I gesture to the naked girl inside his house, who's probably wondering what is going on out here. "You'll always be you."

He seems to absorb my every word, then shakes his head slowly. "You don't get it. You'll never get it. If I can't be with you, Chloé . . ." He shrugs.

"Yeah, I understand. You gotta get it from somewhere, right?" I stare at him.

"You make me sound like a dog," he calls through the drenching rain.

"More like a lecherous Neanderthal."

"That's great, Chloé. Really great."

I have nothing left to say.

He flips up his palms. "I'd quit this all for you. That's what you don't understand."

"So quit!"

"Just give me the word, and I will."

Our eyes lock. I know he means it. I know he'd do that for me, but still I can't make that leap. I'm terrified I'd lose him, and I *can't* lose Rock. I mean, if I lose Gordon it'll suck mongoose, and I'll be hurt as hell, but if I lose Rock . . . I'll have really lost it all. And I have lost enough loved ones for the year—for the decade.

He takes my silence as a sign. His voice is calm. "Chloé, I still love you, but I'm not going to wait around forever. At some point, you're gonna have to decide."

I close the door and pull out of the driveway. My brain feels like fresh roadkill. All screwed up and tangled. As I start driving away, I spot Rock in the rearview mirror, still standing in the doorway, half naked, jeans unbuttoned.

Why is my chest aching? He's right. I'm the one who gave him the red light. I shouldn't even care. Gordon is my boyfriend, not Rock. But I did call Rock my super-luminous giant in the Andromeda Galaxy—always there when I need him.

I would quit this all for you. The words plague me all the way home. Just when I think I know what I want out of life, out of this whole love game—the rules change all over again.

Twenty-four

Try going an entire week pretending nothing's wrong. Try living normally, as if the person you'd given all your energy to for the last three months, and almost gave *yourself* to, didn't act like you don't exist anymore. Try not calling him, even though your fingers itch to. I am so impressed with myself, I can't stand it. On the outside, I may seem fine. *Yeah, me and Gordon are on a little break. We're still good.* But on the inside, I'm dying.

If I tell Rock about my "trial separation" with Gordon, he's just going to say I told you so. And the last thing I want to hear Rock say is I told you so. Why should I give him the satisfaction? Besides, Rock hasn't come to school this entire week. We haven't spoken since our fight, and for the first time in my life, I feel really alone.

At lunchtime, I find Vincent the Dumped sulking on a low wall, popping open a can of Coke. He's not quite a girlfriend, but he's close, since he's such a wuss. I accost him with a shoulder shove. "What happened, Vince?"

"What happened, what?"

I jump up on the wall with him. "I don't know. Just thought maybe something happened."

"You mean with Amber?"

I nod. "I haven't really seen you with her all that much lately."

"Yeah. I haven't seen you hanging with Gordon much these days either."

Ouch. I pick at my nails. "He needs some time. I'm just trying to deal with it the best I can."

He smirks, nodding. "Well, me and Amber just didn't work out. I guess I saw more in her than was actually there."

"We can believe anything we want," I say. And suddenly, I'm wrought with hypocritical guilt the size of Jupiter. I have always tried to see more in my relationship with Gordon than what I originally believed was there. *Is* there really more to us? Or am I just a female Vince, imagining grandeur where there is none?

"Yeah," he says, bringing me back to our conversation. "I'm not going to play her game, Chloé. That girl is full of games." I watch Vincent comb his straight black hair back with his fingers and take a sip from his Coke. I always thought that he was in the same boat as Rock, that he was just looking for a quick, no-strings-attached, fun time. But then I see him press his lips together in that way boys do when they think they might lose it, and I feel for him.

I put my arm around his shoulder. "It's okay, Vince." I pat him gently. "Let her go. You deserve better. There's plenty of other girls out there."

He nods. "Yeah, well, if I ever find one like you, I'll put a GPS on her so I won't lose her."

"Aw, thanks, Vincey-poo!" I laugh, bumping his shoulder in appreciation of the compliment. He takes another sip from his drink.

The hallway has grown pretty noisy. "How do you like working at Gears Auto?" I ask.

"Aw, it's great. I get free and discounted stuff all the time."

"That's awesome," I say, imagining Vince coming home with bags full of cool, new stuff. Motor oil, car-wash stuff, bras (the front covers, not the lingerie), and full car tarps. Wait a minute . . .

"Why are you looking at me like that?" he asks self-consciously.

"Did you . . . ?"

"Did I, what?"

"Vince, did you cover my bike a few months ago with a tarp? One day when it was raining really hard? It was brand-new with, like, creases in it and everything."

He swallows slowly and tilts his head. "Um . . . don't kick my ass, Chloé. I just wanted to help you because she was about to get dumped on really bad."

"So it *was* you!" I should've known. Ambitiously cool,

but utterly uncool Vince. I cannot bring myself to be mad at him. He was only being sweet.

"Don't do that ever again." I softly kick the wall he's on. "My uncle paid a mint for those blue flames. They could get scratched."

"I know. That's why I never said anything. But you realize it could get scratched by not covering it too, right? You know how people here don't give a shit. They totally touch Lolita when you're not looking."

Hmm. Valid point there, King Doof. "So, how much does one of those things cost? I would need a soft one made for motorcycles, not that crap you gave me."

"Sorry. It was the only one I had in my trunk. I'll see if I can hook you up with a better one."

"That'd be awesome. Thanks." I punch his knee.

"Not a problem." He smiles.

What's strange is how all the wrong boys are showing me their appreciation. First Rock, and now Vincent. But not the one I want. Not the one I need. I don't tell Vince about the imploding star that is my heart, or about the street intersection sign wobbling back and forth in my head— Rock ST, Gordon AVE—giving in to the slightest wind that pushes it. On the outside, I am intact and in control.

Last period, trig, and I'm drawing circles.

Then squares.

Then triangles connecting them together.

Mr. Ungar talks, and I pretend to be jotting down everything he says, but all my pencil can draw are shapes. Shapes with little dots at the corners, shapes with stripes in them, polka dots, and little squiggly lines. Soon, I'm drawing hearts with zigzags inside, swords piercing them just like Mom's old Tarot cards. A far cry from trigonometry.

Half the class is in a coma, the other half trying to stay tuned in to whatever Mr. Ungar is talking about. I've never had a problem with trig and I'm not about to start now, or else I'll never see Lolita again.

So . . .

I force myself to sit up and ignore the clock. I fold back the page, pushing the heart-sword doodles out of sight. I start copying the notes from the board.

> Looking at isosceles triangle ABC and the altitude from vertex B to side AC, we have
> $\cos(pi/7) = (b/2)a = b/2a$

Right, I knew that. Gordon would be proud.

I'll use this "break" wisely and study my brain off. Not only will Gordon be impressed with my *superintelligenetic* powers when we get back together, but I'll be one step closer to recovering Lolita, my forbidden ride. Even if this plan fails, I'll have done something constructive with my time. Maybe it'll even make the time go faster somehow.

The bell rings, taking me by surprise. See? It's working already.

With my plan in place, I feel strong, purposeful. I walk the halls quickly, weaving in and out of people all racing one another out of the buildings, heading toward the parking lot.

Impossibility strikes.

I see the giant nerd himself, heading in my direction. Only Gordon would be *entering* the school building as everyone else is fleeing. I want to hide behind a column like a frightened deer. Instead, I make eye contact with him and give him a friendly smile. I'll show him I am not the impatient, overbearing girlfriend he spoke with on the phone last week. I am composed. I will impress Gordon with my high level of emotional maturity.

He waves at me and does a little jog through the hallway mob to reach me. Is this the end of the waiting period? Is he ready to see me again? My heart leaps around.

"Hey, sweetie. What's up?" I ask. His hair is gelled back a little. He looks different. I want to kiss him like the last time we kissed at the dock. In the water, when we almost . . .

Find out what he wants.

"Everything, that's what's up." He looks around the hallway, distracted. "I have two tests this week, a study lab with some guys from calc II, and I've been accepted to take college classes this summer."

Blah, blah. I don't care about any of this. What about me? I just want him to want *me*. "Really?" I fake intense interest. "That's awesome! Where?"

"UM. They have a program for high-school students interested in majoring in engineering. It depends on whether or not my brother's coming home for the summer, funds, a whole bunch of different reasons."

"What about MIT and the early-entrance thing?"

"So many variables, Chloé. All the more reason why I need time to think."

Still? I listen to him explain more about both programs, and I really wish I was more interested, but the only question burning in my mind at the moment is: *Can I kiss you now?*

Maybe my pathetic face betrays me, because he stops and squints. "Are you okay?"

"Yeah, I'm fine," I lie. *Never better!*

"You sure?"

I press my lips together and nod. I want to say, *No, I am not at all okay with this forced limbo, Gordon,* but I keep it together. I don't know how much longer I can hang in there, though.

"Because I really want you to know," he goes on, "that I appreciate all the time we spent together."

Appreciate? I want to spit the word in his face and make him explain why he's talking about us in the past tense as if we're over, finished, when he said he just needed some time. But for whatever reason, I can't bring myself to say anything. Not here with the current of people going by.

I look away and scan the hallway, look at anything but his face. In three months, we managed to go from bickering opposites in a forced situation to two people who understand and love each other. That, to me, is a world of accomplishment. Now he's saying he *appreciates* me.

"How's chemistry?" he asks, changing the subject. If he cared so much about my chemistry grade, he would study with me after school today. It could be our *raison d'etre*, you know, like if all else fails, at least he's still my peer tutor.

"Great. It's going great. I think I'm going to pass after all." Of course, that's another lie, but if I have any hope of getting back with Gordon, he has to see that I'm dedicated, succeeding, taking life seriously, that I have goals. Like him. He cannot, no matter what, see the mess I so clearly am.

"You sure?" He looks down at me. He seems taller today.

Or maybe I'm just shrinking.

"Yeah! Why do you keep asking? Don't you believe me?"

"Of course I believe you." He looks down at my hand. I'm burning for him to take it, give it a squeeze, place it on his heart. "I always have."

I can't take this. I can't take these mixed signals. If he wants me, he should tell me. If he doesn't, he should tell me, so I can move on. I open my mouth to speak. There has to be something that will convince him, that will set him straight on the path to my heart. But what?

"Chloé . . ." he says, before I have the chance to tell him anything. "I know I sprang this break on you, but there's so much on my plate right now, and . . . I just wasn't expecting to have a girlfriend. You took me by surprise. I didn't mean to piss you off the other day, but I need you to understand."

I nod, watching his hazel eyes carefully for any signs of lying. But there's no flickering, no hesitation. He's confused. At least he acknowledged that I threw him off. I smile, proud at my throwing-off abilities. It's the best I'm going to get for now.

"Gordon, do what you have to do. But I want to be with you, to give it a solid try. If it fails, it fails. You make me mad sometimes, but you make me really happy, too. We have something unique, and I know we can make it work, even with your parents. I just want you to know that."

There. All out on the table. Take it or leave it.

He smiles, and as my breathing stops to register the moment, he takes my hand in his. "I understand everything you're saying. Let's talk about it again when school's over."

That's a whole month and a half away! I want to say. My

heart bobs up and down in my chest like a buoy out in the bay. *Focus on the positive. He may want to get back together when school's over.* I break away from his hold before my eyes have the chance to well up again. I will not be a crying wuss. Crying wusses never get what they want.

"Okay, let's do that. We'll talk in a few weeks. Study, study!" I smile and quickly leave him.

I head out of school. No Murphys' dock for me today. Today, I start all over like I did the day I met Gordon. Only this time, I'm really going to do it. I'll play this game right. I won't whine about Gordon anymore. I won't blame outside sources for my knowledge deficiency—not Mr. Rooney, not Gordon, not because I've had nine months of mourning. I will take responsibility this time and find someone who can help me take control.

Even if they are a metal-mouthed, paper-clip-loving *girlgoyle*.

Twenty-five

The following Monday, I sit alone in the computer lab. Mr. Ungar is absent today, so I took the opportunity and asked the substitute if I could come here, claiming I needed to finish research for my nonexistent English paper. Here, one can Google in peace without leaving temporary internet files and cookies for spying mothers to see. I type in FINDING BIRTH PARENTS, and my pulse quickens.

I should not feel guilty about this. Even my mom said she would do it.

I print out at least twenty listings for agencies that investigate closed adoption cases and stuff them into my bookbag. After skimming the first four or five websites,

I realize that I'm going to need some money to get the information I'm looking for. I'll have to get a job this summer and use some of the paychecks for this. If they find that your parents are long dead, I wonder if they return the money.

It's May 1, and peer tutoring has become the mecca for the academically desperate. A few new tutors have joined the cause. The auditorium is louder than ever. No one even notices the loud doors anymore. No one notices me come in.

Sabine stands in the middle of the right-hand aisle talking to a girl with stringy long hair. She sees me, her ponytail swinging hard when her head turns. *Yes, I'm back, even though Gordon's not. Don't rub it in, girly girl.* Sabine goes back to talking. I look for a new seat. The old spot will not do.

Should I ask her now? No time like the present, I suppose.

I put my stuff down and start down the aisle, but just then the girl Sabine tutors, Francine, comes bouncing up the aisle, and they take their seats. Now that I think about it, Francine had a valuable idea there, requesting someone of the same sex. Maybe I wouldn't be back at square one had I done the same.

I want to turn and sit back down. Maybe I could get started by myself today, then approach Sabine next time, but . . . that's procrastinating. The new Chloé procrastinates not.

At Sabine's row, I crouch down. "Sabine," I whisper.

She doesn't hear me, but Francine points at me. Sabine turns to look.

"Hi. Can I talk to you a minute?"

She glances at Francine as she stands. I wonder if they've become friends, if they've talked about me. "Uh, sure," she says, and we stand in the aisle.

"I know this is weird, but I was hoping you could help me."

"With?"

"Tutoring."

"But I'm already tutoring someone."

"Yes, I know that." Why am I asking her anyway? Why not any one of these other people? I notice a few kids sitting cross-legged on the stage talking to Ms. Rath. They're probably tutors too, benched, waiting for the opportunity to play. Still, I can't take my chances with them. "I need you."

"Why me?"

"You know chemistry better than anyone here. Gordon said so," I say, remembering our first tutoring session.

"He did?" She looks surprised.

I nod. "Yes. I know this might seem a little weird, but I need you. I have to pass Rooney's class. And you're really good at helping people," I add to butter her up. "Maybe you could tutor me on another day? My mom could pay you."

She squints and turns her back to Francine, whom I notice is straining to hear our conversation. "Can I ask you something? Are you and Gordon still . . . ?" Her expression is full of curiosity, hurt, and annoyance all at the same time.

"Yes, we're still together. Well, sort of. I think."

"What do you mean?"

I cross my arms. "What does it have to do with tutoring?"

"It doesn't. I just want to know."

"I—"

"Forget it." She starts turning away. "It's none of my business. I'm sorry I asked."

"No, wait." I touch her arm, and she turns back to face me. "What's wrong?"

Her expression softens a bit. "Well . . . Chloé. You're asking me for help, but you realize that Gordon used to be my boyfriend, right? For six months."

"Yes, I know," I say, but I didn't know it was six months. That's longer than us.

"So it would be weird for me to sit across from you and give you help, knowing the history you guys have together now."

"I'm not sure it's much of a history, really. I mean, yes, we hit it off quickly at first, but then he . . ." I think of how to put this without making myself look pathetic. I can feel my face stinging the way it does right before the tears begin.

"Put you on hold?" Her eyebrows rise, and every one of the last conversations Gordon and I had comes rushing into my brain like a flash flood. So it's not just me.

"He did the same to you?" I ask.

She nods.

"Oh," I say for lack of a better response.

"No offense, Chloé, but I was wondering how long it would take with you."

"Well, thanks. That's sweet."

"I don't mean that in a bad way. It just—look—I don't know. I'm not strong enough right now to be able to help you, knowing that you guys were together like that. You don't know how I felt about him," she says, looking around the auditorium uncomfortably.

Yes, I do know.

You fell in love with him just like I did.

And he set you aside, just like he did with me.

"You don't know how it killed me to drive by his house and see your motorcycle out front," she says, her eyes turning pink and glossy.

"I do know how you feel," I say, remembering how it killed *me* to see the unfamiliar cars outside Rock's house.

Oh.

God.

What does this mean? That I'm in love with Rock? God, that is *so* wrong.

"So I guess I can't blame you," I add, staring at the plastic seat buckets. "Don't worry. I'll find someone else." I head for the stage, hearing her apology as if from another dimension. I can do this without Sabine. I never needed anyone before and I don't need anyone now.

Suddenly, I spot my godmother, purse on her shoulder, keys in hand, talking to Ms. Rath up on the stage. "Marraine," I call, giving her a little wave.

She pats Ms. Rath's shoulder as a thank-you, then points at the steps on the side of the stage, where she heads. I meet her there. *"Salut."* I kiss her cheek. "What are you doing here?"

"Cherie, sit down." We sit on the steps.

"What's wrong?" I remember my father's face, pained and tortured, as he approached me in the garage with the news of Seth's death. *It's okay*, linda, *it's okay* . . . he'd said, because he could tell I already knew.

"Nothing is wrong," she says, tucking a strand of hair behind my ear. "I only want to talk. I've been worried about you."

"Why?" I give her a shoulder shrug.

"Chloé. Please. I wasn't born yesterday."

I stare at her bright brown eyes. The lines around them remind me of how long this woman has loved me. A long time. She takes my hands in her beautiful manicured ones. Her long nails are light pink today. "You've been under a lot of stress lately."

"I'm fine." I pull my hands out of hers.

Her eyebrows draw together. "You don't have to say that." She sees right through me. There's no hiding from Marraine. "You're not okay. You've had a hard year, Chloé." The words jab me in the gut because they're true.

I can't answer.

"You lost your uncle, whom you loved," she says. I try to hold back the tidal wave of tears rising against the backs of my eyelids. They're only so strong. She looks at her hands and tries to calm a breath. "Believe me, he loved you very much too. You two were like twins born at different times. I know this."

Brother and sister . . . astral cords bonding us together . . .

"I know you've been at the computer lab," she says slowly.

I shrug defensively. "So? Anyone can use the lab."

"Yes, but I know what you've been looking into."

I never erased the links to the adoption sites. I never thought that anyone using the computer after me would care. "You've been spying on me, Marraine?"

Her shoulders slump. She looks defeated. "Your mother asked me to. The babies take up a lot of time, but she still wants to look after you."

"That doesn't give anyone the right to spy on me."

"*Cherie*, if you're curious about your past, ask your parents, love."

"But they don't know anything. Either way, I'd need to do a professional investigation."

"Yes, but at least they can help you make sure you're not getting taken advantage of. And you're going to need money to do what you're looking into. Chloé, use them to your advantage—they're your *parents*. But if they don't know that your interest is *this* strong, how can they help you?"

I don't know whether to be mad or grateful that I have someone to talk to about this. I love the relationship I have with my parents and don't want to change that in any way, and I thought involving them would complicate matters. And I *hate* complicating matters! I sigh and rest my head on Marraine's shoulder. My eyes start leaking.

"Believe me, I know nothing is easy right now. But even Mr. Rooney will pass you if he sees you working your hardest from now until the end of the year. I'm not supposed to tell you that, but I've known the man for a few years, and I can tell you he's done it many times before."

"I am trying, Marraine. I came here for help from someone else because Gordon's not tutoring me anymore. Coming here wasn't easy for me."

"Well, there you go, then. A little focus goes a long way." She smiles and uses her thumbs to wipe my eyes. "You are a piece of work, Chloé Rodriguez. Now get studying."

I sink into a seat with no desire to start studying, though I know I have to.

She slings her purse back on her shoulder. "Chloé, your mom and dad are stronger than you give them credit for. They'll understand what's on your mind. You have a dedicated family, more dedicated than some 'real' families, as you say."

I press back the tears. "I know," I whisper.

"And if you need me, I'm here too. You never have to face anything alone." I'm not sure why, but those words send me over the edge, and it takes me five whole minutes to get my eyes dry and my face in the shape it was in before she came to see me.

In the morning, guess who's waiting for me as I pull into a regular car spot with my big gray elephant? I step out and squint at her in the sun.

"So here's the deal . . ." Sabine pulls on the straps of her backpack as I turn off the truck and lock up. "Two days a week. Your house after school. We won't talk about Gordon. Okay?"

"Totally."

"I'm sorry about yesterday."

"It's okay. I shouldn't have ambushed you like that."

"You asked me for help, and I gave you a super-hard time. Whatever is going on between you and Gordon is none of my business. I just need to realize that."

"Believe me, not much is going on." I smile.

"But I still don't want to know." She smirks back, and I don't know if it's because we're not in the dull light of the auditorium or what, but she looks different out here in the sunlight. She's so going to look pretty when she finally gets those braces off.

For the next three weeks, Sabine comes over on Tuesdays and Thursdays and doesn't charge my mother anything. She really is, quite possibly, the sweetest person on the face of the planet. I don't understand how Gordon could ever have dumped her. He's an idiot.

The rest of the days, I study all by my determined self—at the dock, at home, even in Rooney's classroom after school to demonstrate my dedicated effort. I study anywhere but the auditorium, locale of the great fateful Chloé-Gordon hookup. I pass every quiz Rooney pops with at least a 70 percent. I talk to no one but Sabine and my family. Rock, I just leave alone to figure things out. And Gordon, I just smile at him in the halls as a silent reminder that I still love him.

Do I miss them? Yes. But Gordon was able to put me aside for his reasons, right? So I can do the same. Even though I'm still counting on that post-school discussion about getting back together this summer. As for Rock, he's been in and out of school this whole time anyway, which means he's probably messing around with someone new, and I don't care who. So much for changing lifestyles for me. So much for us being friends. He's going to have to find himself a guy friend who doesn't mind listening to how he gives himself over and over to girls who don't love him. Until that ends, I can't be a part of it anymore.

At the Murphys' dock, the crickets and frogs perform their nightly symphony. The air is dead, not a breeze to speak about. My shirt clings to my sweaty skin, damp as though it never fully dried after washing. I remember how wet my clothes were that beautiful afternoon Gordon and I were last here together. That day was so perfect. And who had to go and ruin it? Someone whose name rhymes with *crock*.

I look through my adoption investigation printouts. There's one investigator in South Miami, not too far from where I live. It's a woman, and her history reads that she's an adopted child herself. She goes into details about the discovery of her own birth mother and how she finally met her after forty years, but also explained how every case is different and some don't turn out so well. I know this. I'm prepared for this. I still want to go through with it.

I shine my flashlight onto the new sign posted on the property announcing demolition for Monday, June 5—one week from now. It's funny how I feel I can handle meeting my birth mom, yet I don't think I can let go of the dock. So many memories were created here. Most recently, those with Gordon—swimming during spring break, talking at night about space quantum theories, ancient Earth, our world's oldest civilizations . . .

Does Gordon even know what it's like to be put on-hold like this? Has anyone, in his entire privileged life, ever told him to wait, to stand by while they decide how they feel about him? Has he ever been the victim of anyone's doubt?

Probably not. So I *have* to forgive him for doing this to me. Because he just doesn't understand. If he *knew* how it felt, he wouldn't do it.

I turn the flashlight off and wait for my eyes to adjust again.

Betelgeuse seems brighter tonight. So do Arcturus, Regulus, and even Spica. I want to give the stars the dedication they've given me. I want to watch them forever, maybe even reach them one day. If I'm going to spend so much time staring at the skies, I may as well make a career out of it. But I'm pretty sure you need passing grades for that, so I have to keep working as hard as I have. Maybe I can get a job at Miami's planetarium this summer. It'll help pay for the investigation, and hopefully, even a new telescope. Not a cheapie one, but one of those apochromatic babies with the five-inch apertures.

My phone rings the new tune I've added. Sabine. "Hello?"

"Hi, Chloé."

"Hey! I just finished the work you gave me."

"That's awesome. Go, you." She laughs a little.

"Yeah, I think I'm ready for the final. I couldn't have done it without you, so thanks."

"You're welcome." She hesitates. "Do you have a minute?"

"Yeah, what's up?"

"I know we agreed not to talk about Gordon, but considering what you're going through and the fact that I went through the same shit because of him, you should know something."

"What is it?" I ask, amused on the one hand at hearing the word *shit* come from the mouth of Sabine Jimenez, but dreading, on the other hand, that she has news about Gordon.

I can hear her hesitation over the line. I don't know who will take whatever she has to say harder—me or her. "I think he's moving."

I hear her. I do. But it makes no sense. There's no way Gordon could have told everybody about this surprise announcement before telling me, his girlfriend, who loves him, who adores him.

I blink. "Moving to another place in Miami, or . . ."

"No, to Boston," she says.

I do my best to keep my voice calm and my thoughts rational. I bite my lip hard before asking, "He told you this?"

"My friend who's in calculus with him heard him telling Philip."

"Philip?" Of all people. I can hear the blood rushing inside my head, like a broken levee against my eardrums.

"Chloé, if we weren't friends, I wouldn't have told you anything. In fact, I probably would've enjoyed this. But we *are* friends. At least I think so."

"We are," I say, and I do get the sense she's telling me this because she doesn't want to see me clueless anymore, not because she's enjoying breaking the news to me. "Thanks. I'll call you back."

"Chloé?" her voice pleads.

"Yeah."

"Don't be mad at me."

"Of course not."

"It was only fair you should know."

Yup. Got that right. "I know. Thanks, Sabine." I hang up, and for a moment, I just sit there. I imagine Gordon's car pulling up to the dock. He's come over to apologize, to tell me how much he loves me. To say that the time we spent was not wasted. That he's thought things through and wants us to move forward with our relationship. That the news about him leaving isn't true.

But then I'm back in the present, and I know in my heart of hearts that there are truths and there are lies. And I'd have to be stupid, blind, or both . . . not to see which one is which.

Twenty-six

My chest pounds at the sight of his house, the place of our middle-of-school-day trysts. His room light glows in the darkness. My heart is beating between my ears.

Closing the truck door softly behind me, I head up the brick-paved path to Gordon's house. This is the first time I've actually ever rung the doorbell. He's going to be miffed when he sees me. It takes a minute, but the front door finally clicks and opens. A small woman with brown hair pops through. Gordon's mom. "Yes?"

"Hi." I smile like the innocent, smart girl I am. "Is Gordon here?"

"He is," she says, a tinge of Russian z in her s. "But it's eleven o'clock. Can I help you?"

The absurdity of what I'm doing hits me hard. "Oh. I didn't realize the time. I'll call him tomorrow. I'm sorry to bother you." I start heading for the truck.

"Are you Chloé?"

My heart sinks when I turn and see her narrowed eyes. "Yes."

She leans on the door frame. "Do you realize that my husband and I know you've been spending time here while we're not home?"

My body freezes, my eyes glance at the perfectly laid brick pattern of the walkway.

"I wonder if your mother knows about it. Or should I ask her myself?" she asks accusingly.

My eyes glue themselves to hers. Not a moment of regret creeps in to humble me. Her son is just as responsible for our behavior as I am. I have not done anything to corrupt him, if that's what she's suggesting. I accept that I will always seem like a bad influence to some people.

"You have nothing to say?" she asks.

"I wanted to meet you properly," I say slowly. "I've wanted to for a long time now. But Gordon insisted on doing it this way."

"I'm sure my son had his reasons." She looks me up and down like there's something wrong with what I'm wearing.

"Sorry to bother you." I turn around to leave before I blow up on her.

"Mom." Gordon appears at the door in pajama pants and a T-shirt. "I'll handle it."

The usual mixed feelings of anger and elation at seeing him well up inside my throat.

"Be quick. It's late," she says coldly, finally breaking her hard stare at me. Gordon nods and closes the door behind him.

"Great, now I've gone from being a secret to being a problem to be dealt with." I lean against a column, kicking it with my heel.

"Why are you here?" he asks. Not in a rude way. Just seems curious.

"Why am I here," I repeat. "Well, let's see . . . about a month ago, you told me to give you some space because you needed to work things out. But you haven't called, haven't given me any updates . . . nothing. Yet your words gave me all this hope that maybe we'd get back together once school was over. So I'm here because school is almost over, and I think we need to talk about it now."

"But Chloé, this is bad timing. I have finals in a few days."

"*We*, Gordon. *We* have finals in a few days. You're not the only one with important things to do."

He runs his hands through his hair nervously. "I just . . . I still don't know." He shakes his head.

"Don't know what? You keep saying that, Gordon. But I need a better answer."

"You deserve a better answer. I'm just not able to give it to you. I'm sorry, but I'm just not."

I chew on my top lip. "If you don't want to be with me anymore, then just say it so I can move on."

"It's not that I don't want to," he says, looking at me in

the most genuine way possible. "You're incredible, Chloé. You're funny, smart, beautiful . . . I really do love you."

His words slice right through me. I feel my nose flaring from how hard I'm trying not to lose it.

"I always have a great time when I'm with you," he goes on, his face wracked with conflict. "You probably think that's bullshit based on the way I'm acting, but it's not. It's the truth."

"But . . ." I prompt, waiting for the *stellacular* reason why he'd be willing to give up all these great things if they're so true.

He lifts his hand and resigns, letting it fall hard against his side. "But we can't be together."

We can't be together. The words hurt me, yet at the same time, give me insurmountable strength. Truth. Reassuring, painful truth. *We can't be together.* That's my answer. But I knew this right from the very beginning, didn't I? I just didn't listen to the warnings. I knew that Gordon already had a master plan in place and that I was never a part of that plan. More like an interruption.

"Right." My brain tries processing a world of other truths, like that I'll never again feel his kiss on my lips, never again lie in those arms, the ones he's now folding in front of him. Never again will we talk about the things that make me feel important and smart.

"It's not what you think." He blinks softly.

"You don't know what I think," I say softly, shaking my head. Let's see how long it takes him to come clean. I know Sabine's not lying about his moving. I've seen her for who she is now, and I can say that with 100 percent certainty.

"You're right. I don't."

"So what is it, Gordon? I want to hear the big reason why we can't be together if you still love me."

He takes a deep breath then lets it out real slow. "I'm leaving, Chloé. I'm going back to Boston. As soon as school finishes."

He waits for my reaction, but I don't give him much of one. If he really loved me with all his heart, he would try to find a way to stay and be near me. I know that's a very "linear" way to think, but I can't think rationally right now.

"You don't look too surprised," he says.

"I would be, if I hadn't already heard this from someone else." I enjoy the awesome look of shock on his face before continuing.

He covers his mouth, blowing air out against his hand. "I'm sorry."

"You bet your ass you're sorry," I say, feeling the irreversible Chloé come creeping in. "Why are you leaving?"

"Because MIT has a better engineering summer intensive? Because my brother's there, because my dad's original job is there . . . I could give you a million reasons. My dad was managing the regional offices here, but he can just as easily—"

I don't care about his dad, brother, goat, or chickens. "So this is more their decision. You didn't really have a choice in the m—"

"No, it's what *I* want," he interrupts.

Not, "*I have no control over the situation*," but "*It's what I want.*" I try not to let my jaw hang open. "Did you know all this when we were together? When we almost did it at the dock? Or any of the days you snuck me up there?" I point to his room. "In the three months we were together, you couldn't have told me? In the past month I've been *waiting* for you, you couldn't have said something?"

"I didn't want to complicate things while we considered the pros and cons. We just decided for sure."

"Well, hooray for you," I say, because I'm lacking any other brilliant comebacks.

"Chloé," he says slowly. "Remember I asked you not to get your hopes up with me? Remember I tried to warn you?"

"Well, I thought it was a general sort of warning, as in 'We're not good for each other,' which I already knew was bull, because we *are* good for each other. Had you actually said, 'Because I'll be moving this summer,' I might not have let myself get so attached to you. I might not have let myself fall in love with you, but I did, and you didn't do anything to stop it either."

Why does my chest feel like it's splitting open?

"You're right. I shouldn't have strung you along. And I'm sorry I didn't tell you about this sooner. But as much as I love you, care about you, I'm not sure we were really *in love*, Chloé. Maybe we were in love with the idea of being in love. That happens to people all the time."

You know, I should have seen this. There he is, the same Gordon of "to adore means to worship" fame, and he doesn't worship anybody. He made that very clear. That was the real warning right there. The only thing I can manage to say is, "You're right, this love thing was all a part of my evil plan to throw you off course."

"Funny. But you have to admit a big part of your agenda at first was to do just that—to hold me back."

"What? You can't be serious!"

"*Shh.* My mom," he whispers. "Yes, I'm serious, with your 'Let's leave, let's get out of here,' and your pulling me off track when I was supposed to be focusing on my studies."

I ignore his plea for quiet. "Fuck your studies! You had full control of your actions, Gordon. I didn't put a gun to your head. Or did you forget that you were your own person capable of making your own choices? I had to study just as much as you did. For different reasons maybe, but I did."

"Yeah, so you don't lose your motorcycle." He says motorcycle like it's a tricycle.

"Like I said, different reasons."

"And that's my point. Our priorities are different. They've always been. Look, forget it. I'm not interested in hurting you any more than I already have."

"Well, that's noble of you."

For a minute, we're quiet. Yes, our priorities are different, but I thought we had rubbed off on each other and become more balanced people. I know it's my last act of desperation, but I search his eyes, hoping that something—a memory of us at the dock, or in his room, or one of our incredibly long kisses will make him reconsider.

But he just blinks softly, as if waiting for me to make the next move.

"The only thing I ever wanted," I say calmly now, "was for you to smile and be happy. Because, guess what, Gordon? Life is short. And you never know if you'll die tomorrow.

Then all that planning for the future will have gone to waste."

"I appreciate your way of thinking, Chloé, I really do. And I know it stems from your experience with your uncle, but we still can't be together right now. I mean, if you need me for anything, absolutely anything, I'll still be here a few weeks longer, but otherwise . . ."

Slowly, I absorb reality. It's over. "Then this is it."

He reaches for me, but I shy back. "Don't do that, Chloé. I have to know that you're going to be okay."

In his face, I don't see a villain. I don't see a player or an asshole. I see a boy who really cares about me, but at the end of the day, I just didn't make it into his sticky-note organizer of Life Priorities. He's getting back on track.

I nod, rubbing my eyes. "Yeah, I'll be okay," I say. I have no choice. "Don't worry about me, Gordon."

"You sure?" I can tell he's asking more for his own peace of mind than for my benefit.

So many thoughts threaten to spill. How he's giving up too easily, how we should give it a fair chance, how he'll be sorry he let me go when he finds himself alone in his room at night wondering what I'm doing . . . but I know two things. One, that nothing I say can change his mind at this point, and two . . .

I think of Rock when he told me that I would be numero uno on his list and remember the afternoon from hell at his house when he proclaimed steadfast willingness to change his entire lifestyle just for me. Ambitious willingness but noble. *That, Chloé, is loyalty. Not this.*

"Yes, I'm sure." I give him a sad smile. "I'll see you

around, Gordon. We'll keep in touch during our senior year and in college. Maybe even get back together in the future. When the time is right."

Gordon smiles brightly. "See, now, there's an idea. We could do that."

I was being facetious, but that's how clueless Brain Boy is sometimes. I'll never be his highest priority. He'll always have projects to finish, professors to talk to, recommendations to secure. There will always be bigger, greater ambitions that will be more important than me. And I don't have time for boys who don't have time for me.

So I take in the look in his beautiful hazel eyes, then lean forward to kiss him one last time. He leans in to accept it. I can feel a part of him breaking down, a little slice of his thoughts regretting his own decision. And as satisfying as that might feel, I'm finished. Quickly, I turn and head back to the truck.

"Just so you know," I say, opening the door and climbing in, "you might have been in love with the idea of love, but I wasn't. I loved you for real." Then, before he has a chance to see my tears, I close the truck door and back out of the driveway.

Twenty-seven

Saturday morning, I'm having *café con leche* alone at Ricardo's, soaking in the sound of plates and silverware clanking. As much as I have tried to let the whole Gordon thing go, I still think about it way too much. I wonder how I could have been so stupid, how I could have allowed myself to get emotionally attached to him. And don't think I haven't also felt guilty that I was so willing to go the distance with Gordon against all odds, yet I wouldn't do the same for Rock.

Why was that?

If anyone deserved that kind of dedication, it was Rock. Was it because I assumed he'd always be there, whereas with Gordon, I felt him slipping away? *Sigh.* Doesn't matter anymore. Neither of them are around now.

I fill out a preliminary survey form for the South Miami adoption investigator. As soon as I'm done with it, I'm going to give her a call. I figure a Saturday would be better, because I can always leave her a message if she's not in the office and that will give me time to think about this some more in case I regret making contact with her.

My phone rings, and I answer it quickly. It's my dad. "Hey. I thought you were fishing today."

"Not today. Where are you?"

"Studying."

"Where, not what."

"At Ricardo's."

"Oh." He hesitates. Why is he suddenly so concerned with my whereabouts? There's something in his voice. "When are you coming home?"

"What's up, Papi?"

"Nothing. Just . . . don't be out too long, *linda*. It's going to rain."

"Dad, it's May in Florida City. It rains every day." I offer a bit of sarcasm, but I can tell there's something waiting in the wings with him. So even though I'm not finished with the survey form, I pay the bill and pack up.

When I pull into my driveway and see Papi swinging on the front porch instead of puttering around the garage, I know something's not right.

I close his truck up and lug all my stuff over to where he sits. "What's wrong?" I bend down and kiss his cheek.

He rubs his temples. "Go inside. Your mother wants to talk to you."

"Is something wrong?" My face freezes up. The last time he looked this way, it was to deliver the blow.

"No," he coos. "Nothing." He reaches next to him to unlatch the front door for me.

I start to move past him, but suddenly he grabs my arm. Slowly, he pulls me close. He plants a kiss on my cheek and squeezes me tightly. "*Linda.*" His voice is right in my ear, the thumb from his grip caressing my skin. He has a wonderful aura about him. "I love you. Whatever happens, that will never, ever, ever change, you understand?" His face is heavy with something I can't quite place.

All I know is that his expression is killing me. What is it? Are they divorcing? After the number of times I've branded them Über-Couple of the Century? Which one would I live with? What kind of example would they be for someone trying to figure out if soul mates still exist in this world?

I swallow a ball in my throat. "Of course, Papi."

He smiles. "It'll be fine. Go."

I enter the house and head toward the sound of my mother and Marraine talking quietly in the living room.

"Chloé?" my mother calls out.

"I'm here." I round the corner and find them sitting opposite each other on the couch. They both smile nervously when they see me. "Why's Papi outside? Did someone die?" I dump my stuff on the love seat.

Mom folds her hands in front of her mouth. "No. Sit down."

I sink to the floor and sit cross-legged. My gaze bounces

from my mom's face to Marraine's and back. "I've pulled up my grade. It's probably a C or even a B by now. You can check with Rooney on Monday," I tell Marraine.

"I've already spoken to Rooney. You're all caught up in his class," Marraine says with a smile.

My mother laughs a little. "She can do anything she sets her mind to, right, Colette?" she says, and Marraine nods. They look at each other, faint smiles on their lips. I bounce my knees up and down. The tension in here is so thick, it's starting to suffocate me.

"Then can I have Lolita back now?"

"Forget the Harley for a second, Chloé." Mom pushes back her red hair and secures it with a clip. She steals glances at Marraine, but my godmother has taken a sudden interest in her nails. "You never asked about your birth parents when you were little."

Oh, God. Here we go.

No warning, nothing. She found answers. My mother did the adoption legwork for me. My breath escapes my lungs. My nerves hang off her every word.

"Which wasn't surprising," she adds. "Kids accept things so easily. You just accepted the fact that we had no contact with them."

My heart starts pounding inside my rib cage. Do I really want to hear what's about to be said? "What are you telling me?" I ask.

She clasps her hands together and holds them at her mouth, as if praying. "Chloé, we do know something about them—your birth parents—if you still want to know."

"What?" I can't believe I'm hearing this. "But you always said you didn't."

"Well, we've been carrying out their wishes for anonymity. We had no choice. But things got complicated."

"What do you mean? Who *are* they?" I look at Marraine. She is trying so hard to act invisible. My head starts spinning. I'm going to puke.

Mom takes a huge breath and lets it out in a gush. "God, Colette, how the hell do I do this?" Her hands are shaking. Marraine moves to my mother's side, taking her hands in hers, the way she did with me in the auditorium.

First Seth, then Gordon, now this. I'm not sure I can take it, but my heart has already splattered on the floor, so what more harm can be done?

"Papi is outside," she says, "because he's upset. He thinks that once you know what we know, that you won't love him the same way anymore. I have to ask you, honey: Do you think having new information might change the way you feel about him?"

"No, of course not," I say quickly. Because it wouldn't. I could find out that Papi is wanted in fifty states for murder and it wouldn't change the fact that I love him. Nothing would.

"Good, because your father—your biological father— changed his mind toward the end, and wanted you to know."

Pause.

"Toward the end of what?" I ask, looking at my mom, then at Marraine, then back again at my mom. She just sits there, as if a telepathic message is going to pop from her head into mine. What is she saying? *Your biological father . . . toward the end . . .*

"Chloé, baby." She closes her eyes, white knuckles clasped in front of her face. Suddenly, her face turns serene, like all fear has just left her, replaced by purpose and peace. She opens her mouth to speak, but I sit back.

Because I already know.

Your biological father.

Toward the end . . .

"Seth." The name comes out of me softer than a whisper. And a giant volcano rises up from the ground, pierces through my chest, and erupts in my heart, spewing lava and fragments of my soul all over the ground. I feel split open, raw.

I can't speak.

I can't anything.

It's the same way I felt at his funeral when I couldn't squelch the squeezing pain in my heart, couldn't breathe, couldn't imagine how I was supposed to live without his jokes, his laugh, how I was supposed to enjoy anything ever again.

My mother's head falls right into her hands. She has no reason to be crying. *I'm* the one who should be crying. She looks different to me, for some reason. It's as if I'm here, she's miles across from me, and still frames of my life with Seth are all spread out between us.

Jumping on his back every single time he'd walk through the door. Tickle fights. Learning to drive the truck. Putting Lolita together, piece by piece. Bragging about him to all my friends how he was the coolest uncle in the world. So young, full of life and fun.

Seth.

I knew this.

One way or another, I already knew this.

"He was fifteen, Chloé." My mother tries to talk through tears, but her sobs catch her breath.

"It's okay, *cherie*." Marraine pats her hand. I stare at them and listen to our neighbor's dog bark outside.

Mom takes a deep, cleansing breath. I want to get up and run to my room or out of the house, but I hold it together. Why didn't he tell me this before? To my face. I had him in front of my face and in my arms.

"He wasn't old enough to raise you, and he didn't want Grandma to, because he wanted you to have brothers and sisters when you got older, so he picked me. Me and Papi."

I gather up enough energy to speak. "And my mother?" I ask, and Marraine looks up with interest. "Don't tell me it's you."

"*Non*." Marraine smiles through tears. "Though that would've been an honor for me, sweetheart."

"Yes, I'm sure Sethie would've liked that." My mother tries smiling. I remember how Seth loved flirting with Marraine, though she always scoffed at him, kind of like me and Vince.

A baby wails out of the kitchen monitor. Marraine leaves to handle it. I hear some shushing, then quiet humming, as the squeaks from the rocking chair chirp out from the speaker.

My mom sniffles, wipes her eyes with the back of her hand. "Your mother's name is Tina Norris. She had brown hair and blue eyes. She was Sethie's girlfriend for, like, a month. You have her exact face."

I imagine a girl like me, arms around a swollen belly, pregnant after less time than me and Gordon were even together. Missing pieces from my seventeen years come effortlessly flying into place.

"She was fifteen too, Chloé." She pauses to let that sink in. "She went through with the pregnancy, then left you with Seth. He did his best to be a man, but he wasn't a man, honey. He was only a kid—two years younger than you are now. Please don't be angry with him. He did the right thing. He didn't abandon you."

No, he didn't. Or did he? I blink for the first time in minutes, my eyes completely dry. *I'm just like Seth, right, Mom?* I'd always ask. *Yes,* she'd replied so many times over the years, glassy eyes holding back a world of secrets. *Just like Seth.*

"He was going to tell you the day the doctor thought a bone-marrow transplant might work for him. Remember how they took a blood sample from you?"

I nod, the memory of that discussion in the hospital slowly coming back to me. I hadn't understood how I could possibly help.

"Since they were considering you for his donor, he knew he first had to explain things to you. But then he fell into the coma that night, and . . . he never had a chance, baby. I'm sorry."

Sorry.

Connected by astral cords . . .

Like twins born at different times . . .

No, he didn't abandon me. He was always there. Within my reach.

And my birth mother, his girlfriend, was younger than I am now. "Where is she?" I ask, trying to recall every thirty-three-year-old woman I've ever seen in Florida City. Have

I seen her without realizing it? Was she the woman who worked the register at Gears Auto when I was little? Was she the other waitress at the Pancake House?

"Your mom?" my mom asks through fresh tears. "We don't know. She left you with Seth two weeks after you were born. She lived in a world of hurt, Chloé. Very abusive parents, very unstable home. For a while, we tried contacting her, but after a couple of years, we just gave up. We were giving you a better life than she could have anyway, and honestly, I feel that's how it was meant to be."

I nod. I'm not sure if I agree with that or not, but I'll take it. For now.

"We could help you look into it, though, if you still want."

"I don't know."

"I'm so sorry, baby." Her voice is soft and pure. My mother's voice, the only mother's voice I've ever known. "That should never happen to anyone."

Even though I've never felt sorry for myself about this, she's right. It should never happen to anyone. No one's mother should ever abandon them; it doesn't matter how young a mother you are. Maybe I've been angrier about this than I realized, but right now, I don't know where to go from here.

"It's okay," I say, tearing my eyes away from hers. "It wasn't your fault."

I sit there a minute trying to keep it together, but I just want to run. I want to plow out of the house and think about all this on my own, without her staring at me.

"Are you okay?" my mother asks. Then, for the first time in my entire life, I realize something new. I look into her eyes.

"You're my aunt." I hear my voice. It sounds like someone else's.

She nods uncomfortably. "Yes, Chloé. We're related."

She's family.

They were all my family. All along.

Oh, my God. For the first time in my conscious reality, I look straight at a real blood-and-bones relative. A short laugh bursts out of me from the sheer awesomeness of it.

"But for all intents and purposes, young lady, I am still your mother." She laughs forcibly, the way someone does when they're trying to get you to cheer up. "And if you start calling me anything other than Mom, you'll be grounded," she says, starting to cry again.

"What else would I call you . . . Veronica? Even if Tina showed up on our doorstep, I'm always going to call you Mom."

She presses back more tears with her hands. As if this changes how I feel for her. This fills in a lot of holes. Like why we share the same auburn highlights, the same light brown eyes. Because she's my father's sister. I should feel relieved. I should feel *thrilled* knowing all these answers, but in a way, I'm even more fragmented than before.

Mom wipes her face and looks straight ahead, a slight smile at her lips. "I can't believe he missed seeing the babies. He would've loved them." She turns to me and smiles.

I nod.

I would do anything to clear this up with a long ride on Lolita. I want to laugh, cry, scream out loud. But I stand, letting my arms drop at my side. "Well, unless you have more shockers for me, I'll be going."

Where, I have no idea.

"Honey, don't be angry."

"I'm not."

"You started researching and becoming more curious."

"I know."

"And he always wanted you to know one day. Sometimes, I used to watch you two together and feel like I should've convinced him to keep you. To be a father. To work it out. But I knew him, Chloé. My little brother didn't have two ounces of responsibility in him. The most responsible thing he ever did was hand you over."

She covers her face with her hands. I know I should console her in some way. This couldn't have been easy on her, either. I go over to her and sit next to her, leaning my head onto her shoulder. She puts an arm around me and touches my head with hers. This doesn't mean I'm fine with everything, because I'm not.

"Can I take the bike now?" I know it's so beside the point, but it's all I can ask.

She laughs, pretends like she is pushing me away. "*Augh*, you and that bike." She gets up and heads for the kitchen, wiping her face with a dish towel. She doesn't answer my question.

"Can I?" I ask again.

"I'd rather you didn't." I think she's going to say something else, but she doesn't. That wasn't a yes.

It wasn't a no, either.

Twenty-eight

For hours, I sit in the dark garage, surrounded by the mixed scents of motor oil and fishing tackle. I feel like I should cry or something, but who can shed tears when surrounded by such loveliness? I cradle my helmet in my lap and watch Lolita.

Seth was my dad.

Of course he was.

Why didn't I listen to my instincts and figure it out sooner?

Now I can't get him back, can't run to him, can't tell him that I know his secret, can't ask him all the questions burning inside my head—like how am I supposed to see my baby brothers as brothers now, and not cousins? Should I keep the secret going just for them?

Life sucks. But it could always be worse. Still, it sucks.

And I can't control it any more than an electron can. Because that's all I am. A tiny particle trying to reckon with the universe's larger plan. A chip of ice caught in a massive planet's orbiting current, along for the ride.

The only light in the garage is the tiny orange circle of the door opener. I stare at it. *Open.* And since I'm newly dedicated to listening to my heart more, and since maybe Gordon was right when he said I'm a rebel without a cause, unable to stay home while vortices of thoughts spin around in my head—I stand and press it.

The metal garage door springs to life, slowly sliding open like the giant shutter of a weather observatory, exposing the spreading sheets of gray rain clouds dominating the sky. I can't control my life any more than I can control how I feel. And right now, all I want is to fly.

Down the open road.

With the wind and water.

Under piercing bullets of rain.

I set my helmet down on a storage box. Won't be needing it. What's the worst that could happen? I die in an accident and join Seth in heaven the way it should've been all along? No braid, no restraints. Nobody telling me what I can and cannot do. Today, I'm my father's daughter. Today, I'm Motor Girl.

I insert the key and wake Lolita.

We ride through the slicing downpour.

Past cars going too slow, with passengers who gawk at me as

I speed by. Past highway patrol cars, officers shaking their heads, as if they know anything about me. How many of them have just discovered their life has been a lie, I wonder. A beautiful lie that will now change their emotional landscape forever?

The heat from Lolita warms my bones, her vibrations making the hundreds of water droplets on her smooth frame and on my jeans disappear into thousands of tiny droplets in the air.

I head up the Turnpike into Miami, where Seth is buried. The rain dies down to a soft patter. I pull into the cemetery and round the curvy road that tries to make people feel at peace about where they are, that fools them into thinking that their loved ones are in a better place. But I'm sorry, there's no way underground is better than on an open road, wind blasting your face.

I have not been here since the funeral. When there was no stone yet. Only a hole in the ground as we all stood and stared at the sleek brown casket lying inside it.

As my parents drove away, I saw the men come and start filling it.

Now there's a tombstone. I cut off Lolita's engine and take slow steps toward it. It's nice and new, like it was recently put in. It's not one of those pretty ones that stands up but the kind that lies flat on the ground. It's covered in freshly cut grass, wet and sticky from the rain. I run my boot over it to uncover the stone:

IN MEMORY OF
DONALD SETH ALLMAN
BELOVED SON AND FATHER

There. Confirmed in all its marble-etched glory.

He always wanted you to know one day.

Father.

To Chloé Lynn Rodriguez. Or is it Chloé Lynn Allman?

The tears fill my eyes so that I can't see the name anymore anyway. Suddenly, I remember why I haven't come here since he died. Because I can no-way, no-how handle this.

It's like a fissure in my chest wall has suddenly cracked open from the pressure. In my mind, I see fragments of someone who could have been more. I see Seth laughing out loud, his carefree look as he takes off on Lolita down the empty street. I see him withering away in his hospital bed, nurses trudging in and out, his silent eyes holding back secrets I could never have imagined.

I see him watching TV in his tiny trailer, smoke curling around his face, having a beer, never caring about anything other than riding, friends, and riding with friends. And me. I see him holding a wrapped bundle of a baby, not knowing what to do with it. Handing her over in such a way that he would always be near.

Cowardly? Or unconditional, unselfish, undying love?

I see him lying in the funeral parlor. It wasn't him, just wasn't. There's no way he would've ever done his hair that way. I couldn't come all the way up to him, although I wanted so much to fix the lacquered locks on his forehead. On some days, I wish I had, just so I could have said good-bye properly to his face.

Suddenly, I see it all, feel it all, everything that's inside of me, and in one, chest-burning scream, I let it out. I cover my face with my hands. I thought I'd feel closer to him here, but honestly, if I were Sethie, and my spirit could pick one place to be, it wouldn't be this sad, lonesome place. It'd be where the wind and asphalt were.

I lie down in the grass and press my face against the stone. I know the ground is soaking wet, but so am I. I don't care. Even if his spirit isn't here, at least his body is, and that's something. I imagine he's listening as I tell him that I know his secret. That I know it must have been hard for him. That he was stupid for not telling me. I tell him about Gordon, losing the bike, the dock, the situation with Rock . . . and how I feel like I'm on the verge of coming down. Like the Murphy house.

I apologize for having no flowers or offering to leave behind. Not that he would have cared. I let my tears slide down my face and drip into the grass. I imagine them trickling through the earth, past the layers of soil, ants, and chinch bugs . . .

Down . . .

Down . . .

Coming to rest on the smooth, cold metal of his casket. A part of me there to keep him company.

And when I close my eyes, I can almost hear him speak the words I know he would've said to me. Cheesy, fortune-cookie clichés from someone who would know.

Gotta keep going, Chlo.
Don't let anything stop you.
You stop, you die.
So just ride, baby.
Ride.

Twenty-nine

Down US-1, through the Keys, against my parents' wishes. I just ride and ride until the sky turns purple and the watery horizon of the Gulf swallows the sun. The sunset is spectacular, the sky ablaze with orange and yellow clouds. This is what motorcycles were made for. Passing your boundaries. Entering new territory. Throwing it all up in the air to see where it will land.

My cheeks are burned by the wind, and my hair is probably a tangled rats' nest by now. But I don't care. It'll give me something to do later. I'm not worried about my parents. I know my mom's called twice, but I'll call her back later. I just need to be alone right now to clear my head.

Downshifting to third, then to second, I stop at a light in Islamorada, trying to ignore the coughs and sputters Lolita's serving up. Seth would've yelled at me by now. He never would've let her go this long.

As much as I hate admitting to that.

Two old ladies in a Buick pull up next to me. More gawkers.

What?

They look away.

I think of Gordon for some reason. He can go back to Boston, Siberia, or Antarctica, for all I care. It's only been a week since I spoke to him on his front steps, but I'm already used to him being gone. It was good to hear him say that he'd be there for me if I needed him, though. Unlikely that I'd take him up on it, but good. I try to hold down a tidal wave rising in my chest.

An hour of lonely miles goes by, but I have no intention of stopping. The night is darker than burnt motor oil. Stars flicker like cheap little rhinestones. As much as I try to reach them, they keep eluding me, leading me farther and farther down the highway. Where, I have no idea.

My eyes grow so wet, I can hardly see.

Within another hour, I'm somewhere between Marathon and Key West. I've never been this far south without Seth, without a car, without a helmet or riding jacket before. I am so bare right now.

Maybe I'll ride until I fall off the last key, past the southernmost point, just wade right into the Florida straits, past sharks and stingrays, all the way to Cuba. I'll wake up and find myself on the white sugary beaches Papi's grandma always told me about. Nobody would ever know where I escaped to. Nobody would ever find me. Maybe my biological mom is there too. Tina, basking in the sun, avoiding responsibilities, living a life of complete personal freedom.

I think about that.

Tempting.

But my mother—my real mother back home—would never again live in peace, wondering what happened to her child, the one she raised, the one she loved with all her heart, as though she were her own flesh and blood. Gone. Disappeared without a trace like the spoiled, ungrateful brat that she is.

And I know right away that I could never do that. I can fantasize, escape down this way, sulk, cry, and complain all I want, but I could never leave her. In some crazy way, maybe Tina Norris *was* being responsible by leaving me behind. Like Seth, she knew she couldn't handle being a parent. But my folks—my folks took over their parental responsibilities like it was their destiny.

That is some shit right there.

A memory flashes through my mind. It's of me and Seth when I was about nine or ten. We were on the couch, and I was counting the red hairs in his chin versus brown ones while he watched TV. I remember Papi coming in from the garage and stopping when he saw us. He blinked in this slow sort of way, and I thought it was because he liked what he saw: niece and uncle hanging out together.

But now I think it was more.

Was Papi jealous of Seth? Angry at him? Or both? Did he

love Seth as much as I did? How weird it must have been for him to always have Seth around, constantly reminding him that he wasn't my father—not really.

I owe him. Hugely.

Finally, about two and a half hours after leaving the cemetery, I reach Key West, the southernmost point in the continental United States. I break left at the first light and hear Lolita's cough worsen. *Hang in there.* I ride to the public beach and pull into a parking lot to give her a much-needed rest. An hour here and hopefully, she'll be good to go again.

Stretching, my joints crack and my muscles ache, but it's a good sort of ache. Crossing the street onto the beach, I revel at the fact that I am the only one here at eleven o'clock at night. I have the end of the island chain all to myself. The open sea all for me.

My phone buzzes again, but I don't reply. I just lie back on the sand, staring up at the universe. The skies are even darker here than at the Murphys'. "Orion, Cassiopeia, Gemini, Ursa Minor . . ." I name the constellations to myself, then I name them again. I name them for an hour, while the waves ebb and flow five hundred times and my phone buzzes twice more. But I can't look at it.

Seth was my dad.

The *obviousity* of it kills me. I should've held him tighter. Should've kissed his cheek a thousand more times. *Father. Papi. Seth . . .* I drift away.

A cough startles me out of my half sleep. I lift my head and focus in the dark. There's a man there. Standing on the beach to my left, about thirty feet away. Wearing a white long-sleeve shirt, baseball cap, and jeans. Fortysomething, paper bag in his hand. Watching me. Either he's drunk, has lost his ball bearings, or . . . he's evil. I had pushed thoughts of getting into an accident out of my head on the way down, but getting murdered on an empty beach had not once crossed my mind.

Rock's voice comes out of nowhere to warn me. *How did you know it was me and not some crazy freak here to murder you?*

The man keeps watching me. I look away. I may stare back at old ladies on the highway like a bad mofo, but this is different. A silent signal goes off somewhere in my head. Instinct kicks in, and I realize if I don't leave now, I may end up on the news tomorrow morning. This is not how I want my life to end. If I can help it, I would like to live until I'm nice and old, still riding Lolita with my grown children riding alongside me.

I force myself up, and in one swift move, I'm in a standing position, trying not to stumble on the wavy sand. The man comes closer. I don't know what his problem is. He could be good or bad, he could need my help, or he could use a dollar, but it does not matter, because I am not going to find out.

Walk, walk, walk, sand flipping left and right, my feet shuffling faster and faster. I look over my shoulder and pray that he's not following me. He's still standing there, still watching me but not quite following. I jog the last few feet to where Lolita rests, not giving a shit if I look scared now. I notice a pickup truck in the parking lot that wasn't there when I arrived. Why did I have to channel Seth and ride all bad-ass by myself to faraway places? Why, why, why, why?

Swiftly, I straddle the leather seat, insert the key and twist.

Lolita doesn't respond.

"Fuck."

I turn the key again. "I'm sorry about the leak, just please, please . . ."

Nothing.

The man on the beach starts heading my way. I mumble under my breath. "What does he want? What the hell does he want? Come on, Lola."

Don't wait until you break down.

Yes, Papi.

I try again, but Lolita has had it. I didn't take care of her properly, and she's teaching me a lesson. Now, of all possible moments, when there's a strange man headed this way who probably wants to kill me. I don't want to leave her here, but I know when to value human life more than machinery. Yesterday I would've fought for Lolita, done anything to protect the last living piece of Seth. But today, everything's changed.

I am the last living piece of Seth.

I jump off the bike and run.

"Where you going?" the man calls in a gravelly voice. A harmless man would not ask where I am fleeing to. His hands are in his pockets, another detail I don't quite like. I run along the length of the sidewalk under the streetlights. The stupidity of coming here alone slaps me hard.

I run about fifty or sixty feet before slowing down to look back.

The man has reached Lolita and is running his hands along her body, gripping her handlebars. "Nice bike. 'Sit yours?" He smiles.

"What do you want?" I yell, walking backward now.

I watch in horror as he mounts Lolita and pretends to ride her. "*Vrrr, vrrrrruunngg*," he grunts, laughing between fake motor sounds. Yes, he must be drunk. He's lost it too. This must be the gathering place for all who've lost it. But I've already had my taste of self-pity, and now I need to get home. My situation, whether I like to admit it or not, is not that bad.

Where do I go? I left without my license, without anything, and I already used my few bucks for gas. Now I'm here with nothing but my phone. I look down at it. Admitting I need help sucks. Especially on the terms we last left off.

But I call and wait. He said he'd always be there for me.

After one ring, his voice comes on the line. "Where are you? Your parents have been looking for you everywhere, and I've been calling and calling."

"In Key West. I need help," I say, noticing the unsteadiness in my voice.

"What the hell are you doing in Key West, Chloé?"

"It's a long story." I keep my eyes fixed on the stranger on my bike. "Can you make it?"

"Of course I can make it. But it'll take me two hours."

I knew that, but I still want to cry. "I'll wait. Call me when you're closer."

"Jesus . . . all right . . . I'm leaving now, I'll call you in a little while to check on you. Bye."

I hang up and press my phone against my forehead. "Bye," I say to no one.

The man still watches me, his hands all over Lolita. He waves his arms around, all crazy-like, then points to the pick-up truck as if he's offering me the chance to leave with him. When I respond with a bitter finger salute, he acts surprised, fumbles with his keys, gets off Lolita, and climbs into his truck.

Where's the highway patrol when you need them?

It doesn't seem like he's going to harass Lolita any further. The man starts his truck and pulls out of his space. Then he drives away slowly without his lights on, braking every few seconds.

"Leave. There you go." I watch as he makes a left out of the parking lot and drives down the street, turning into a residential area. *Please don't come back.* My legs feel like they're going to buckle, but I can't stay here. I have to keep walking. I dial 911 and have my thumb ready on CALL just in case I need it. Across the street, the houses sit dark. It's late. I'll head down the street, find a Circle K or something.

I don't know what else to do. It's almost midnight. It's been a long day, and it's not over yet. I'm drained. The urge to lie down in my own bed in my own house suddenly washes over me like a tsunami. I'm lost, so far from my life. I know my own stubbornness is what got me here, but right now, I just want to go back.

I think of Papi, probably staring into darkness, unable to sleep, wondering where I am. He must be feeling tortured. He didn't want me to know about Seth, and now I do. He probably thinks I'm going to love him less. He probably thinks I won't regard him as my dad anymore, but that's impossible. If anything, I have two dads, just like one can have two aunts or two uncles, even though I'm sure he didn't want that either. Exclusivity is a beautiful thing.

I sit against a locked-up beach rental hut and call Papi. He answers right away. "Are you okay?" he asks without even saying hello.

"Yes, I'm fine." I'm not really, but help is on the way, and I don't want to alarm him. I watch as a scruffy gray cat crosses the street and stops right in front of me. Its eyes flash at me then it scurries off. It takes a minute, but I realize the silence on the other line is my dad breaking down. "Papi?"

Sniffling noises. His voice is broken. "I'm here."

"I just wanted to tell you . . ." I think about the real reason I called. I don't know that I'll ever find the right words, but I do my best. "That as much as I loved Seth, I love you more. You chose to love me even though I wasn't yours, which I think is harder than having no choice but to love me. Does that make any sense?"

More sniffling, then he clears his throat. "Yeah."

"You raised me, so . . . *you're* my dad."

"I get it. Thanks, *linda*." I know he's wiping his eyes with his arm. I saw him do it at the funeral. "*Augh*," he says through a stuffy nose.

"I'll be home soon. I promise."

"You'd better be home soon," he grunts, and my heart soars.

Thirty

The lost drunk guy doesn't return. But that doesn't make me feel any better. What does make me feel a whole lot better is a sound I hear less than two hours later. I sit up from leaning against the beach rental hut and listen in the windy dead of night.

From behind the sound of the crashing waves comes the rumble of a car engine. It could be anyone driving down the beach, except it's not. It's a deep guttural sound I know all too well. A moment later, bright headlights round the corner, and the high beams flash. I stand and walk over to the road.

He's here.

I wave my arms.

The '68 black Ford Mustang stops where Lolita is parked. I run over to meet him. I want to jump and cry at the same time, but I just stop and watch as he gets out of the car. "What the hell happened to your hair?" Rock asks, staring at me.

I shrug.

"And where's your helmet?" Rock looks around. When I shrug again, he shakes his head and shuts his door. Nothing like someone you love showing up at two in the morning to chastise you for being stupid.

Rock goes to his trunk and starts pulling out an assortment of things—synthetic Amsoil oil, a portable oil extractor vacuum chamber, spark plugs, and a dirty rag. "We should have fixed that leak a long time ago," he mumbles, patiently kneeling by my bike. His arms strain and flex with each pump. Seeing him in his white tank and shorts, I feel guilty for getting him out of bed. Guilty, but glad. "Right now, I'm just gonna change your oil and get her good enough to drive home. Then we can fix the problem when we get back."

"Okay," I say. "I'm sorry for making you drive all the way here."

He lets out a gushy breath, his cheeks inflating on both sides of his mouth. "You still don't get what I'd do for you."

Pump, pump, pump.

"I have a vague idea."

He glances up, and though he's not exactly smiling, he's not entirely mad at me either. He inserts the vacuum tube into the oil tank and opens up the valve. In seconds, the vacuum begins sucking black sludge out of poor Lolita.

"I can't believe I neglected her this long." I lean on the

Mustang and rub my eyes. This has been the weirdest night of my life.

Rock snorts, eyes me sideways. "Maybe you had to neglect her a bit to appreciate her."

Yes, okay, I get it.

He stands and checks out his handiwork. In ten minutes, we'll have a nice clean oil tank to replenish. If she still doesn't start, then we'll have to call a tow truck. Rock comes over to lean next to me on his car. He folds his arms, looking out at the beach. "The Russian dude dumped you, didn't he?"

"He didn't *dump* me," I say, even though he did so dump me. "But let's just say I should've seen it coming."

"Mm-hmm," Rock mutters.

I bump him with my hip. "Yes, I know, I know. No need to say anything."

A minute goes by, and I think he's going to ask more questions about Gordon, but instead he says, "You still think I'm a lecherous Neanderthal?"

I look down at my nails. They're black and the tips are jagged. "Honestly? Sometimes."

"That hurts, you know."

"I know, Rock. But there's a certain degree of truth to it, and it scares me."

"Then I guess I'll be taking off now." He pretends like he's leaving.

"No." I pull his arm toward me, lean my head on it. "Don't." I pout like a baby. After all, I acted like one by not talking to him for almost a month. Even though he's still a lecherous Neanderthal.

"Oh, no? And why not?"

If I say it, the floodgates will open. But I think it's okay now. "Because I need you." There, I said it.

"Oh, now you need me? But I'm a Neanderthal, and you need culture . . . arts . . ." He raises his other arm high in a grand sweeping gesture. "Academia!"

I punch his stomach. "Stop."

His eyelids fall flat. "I thought I wasn't your soul mate. I thought getting together would mean Armageddon for you."

I mumble low into his shoulder. "I don't know what to feel right now. But I do know that true love isn't convenient."

"Huh? I can't hear you."

"I said . . . true love isn't convenient. It happens whether you want it to or not." I stare up at his perfectly formed lips. From now on, I'll try not to think about who else they have kissed. I'll just be glad he wants to kiss me now and no one else.

"What changed, Chloé? I don't want to be second in line just because it didn't work out with that freaky dude."

I ignore that last part. "You're not second in line. But I was. To Gordon. And I never want to be someone's side project."

He twists my hair into a tight coil. "You don't deserve that."

"I want someone who would stop everything he's doing to come and be with me," I go on, very obviously describing someone we both know. "Someone who thinks the world of me the way I think the world of him. But I don't want to lose him either." I look at him, making sure he gets what I'm saying.

He lets go of my hair and stays quiet for a while. Unusual for Rock, but I like it. The wind has picked up in the last half hour, and the waves crash stronger now.

"You don't have to say anything. I know what you're thinking." That I can't have it both ways. That I have to take a risk, and if it works, it works. If it doesn't, it doesn't. I lean into him. His body accepts it. He's not too mad at me.

"I missed you," he whispers, putting his arms around me. "I'm sorry I was stupid."

"I'm the one who was stupid this time." *Stupendicularly* stupid. "You, you're always stupid."

I can feel him smiling even though my face is pressed against his neck. I pull back and look at him. "Promise me something."

He holds his hands up. "Sorry, Chlo, I can't not rag on the Russian dude."

I grin. "No, not that. Something else. Please don't move away or die anytime soon. I don't think I can deal with more bad news."

"Haven't I always told you, you can't kill a bad weed?"

My smile gives in to a quiet laugh. I feel happier and worse than I have in a long time.

"I'll be around." He takes my hand and puts it to his chest. His hand is wider than Gordon's. I've held it before, but it's been a while. My stomach jumps around nervously. I can't believe I'm thinking of taking this risk with Rock.

All at once, I'm hit with exhaustion, overwhelmed by the day, feeling like I've been awake for an eternity, and I start losing the grip on my tears. They well up and spill over, as I think about Seth and about Papi and what he was feeling tonight when I called him. I probably love him more now than I ever did before. He took a risk. He was brave.

I can do the same.

"I need to know that you won't want anyone else, Rock, that you won't have eyes for anyone else. If you can promise me that, then I'm game." I have to know I'm the end of the road. No more flavors of the week, no more Amber. If he can't handle that, this is over before it even begins.

"Chloé . . ." He takes my hand, traces the outline of my fingers. "Did I ever tell you this? One time after I came home from playing at your house, my dad looked me right in the eye—I'll never forget it—and told me that I was going to end up marrying you one day?"

"You never told me that." I smile. "What did you say?"

He wraps his arms around me. "Ew," he says softly by my ear. "I said, 'Ew.'"

My sobs catch a burst of laughter, turning it into a hiccup. His laugh quietly vibrates against my body. With his arms wrapped around me, I feel safe, secure. He lifts my chin and kisses me, soft at first, but then hot, yet reassuring at the same time. I never should've thought of losing my stupid V-status with anyone but Rock.

After a minute, he pulls back to get a good look at me. "You know I don't make promises. Except for you. You hear me?" His face is solid. No smiles. No laugh lines.

I nod, believing him but also knowing it's not going to be easy. Rock is Rock, and people don't change overnight. However, I know that he will try his hardest for me. I'm more sure about this than anything else right now.

"So now . . ." he says. "Tell me again why I've come to

rescue your sorry ass all the way down here at the end of the freakin' world?"

"I had to get away for a while."

"And you couldn't have gone to the dock, or to Ricardo's?"

I shake my head against his chest. "No. This required a much longer ride. My mother just told me who my birth parents were."

If my parents decided it was okay to put *Loving Son and Father* on Seth's stone at the cemetery, then I guess it's no longer a secret. I can't believe I'm about to say this to another soul.

He waits, eyes expectant.

"It was Seth."

I saw Rock's face in the playground the day after his mother announced she was leaving to live with her boyfriend. I saw it when I told him that Seth had slipped into a coma. And I saw it when I told him that Seth's body had finally given up. And nothing, repeat—nothing, has ever made his mouth drop right open like this.

"I freakin' knew it!"

I give him the low-down on Seth, informing him there was no way he could have freakin' known it. Then, we load up Lolita with some fresh motor oil, cross our fingers, and wait. Rock turns the key, presses the starter, and a few guttural explosions burst from the exhaust. He twists the accelerator to get her going. *Vroom . . . vroom.* Seth's voice explodes in my head. *Yeah, baby!*

"You're up and running."

"Yes!" I hiss, hugging him so hard, it hurts my arms.

"Rock, you don't understand . . . I thought I was going to die out here."

He reaches into his trunk and pulls out his big blue comforter. "But we're not driving home now. We're going to sleep. Come on." He slams the trunk shut. Comforter under one arm, he grabs my hand with the other. We stop at Lolita's side to cut her engine and take the key.

"I'm not sleeping on that thing. Who knows where it's been?" Our feet hit the sand.

"It's either this or the sand up your butt."

"I'll take the sand up my butt."

He makes a scandalous face. We flip through the sand until we're close to the water's edge. Then we spread out the comforter. I've spent the night with Rock before, but always as friends—him in a sleeping bag in my room. Never like this, together under a starry sky. Things will be different from this point on. The light is so green now.

Epilogue

I pull on my shades, open the garage door, and let in the morning sunshine. Rock is there, asleep on my front porch swing. "Do you ever sleep at home?"

He opens one eye, then sits up straight. "Ready to get your butt whupped today?"

I fasten my helmet and ease Lolita outside. "Why are you answering my question with a question?"

"Does a girl on a bike stand a chance against this superior piece of machinery?"

"What's wrong, scared to lose?"

He *humphs* quietly, opening his car door. "Let's roll, then."

I lead the way, Rock following me close behind. When

the road opens to two lanes, he passes me and slides to the right, I pass him, then he passes me again. Our little ballet. But then I remember what day it is. I gesture for him to follow me down a different route from the one we usually take.

He turns up his palm outside his window, like, *Where are we going?*

I lead him past the Turnpike entrance, strawberry and onion fields blurring by. This won't be easy, but I said good-bye to Seth and I said good-bye to Gordon, so I know I can do this. A mile later, I turn onto the Murphys' street, gun it down the road, and thrill at the dip. Rock punches it right behind me, and we careen right into the property, kicking up a huge gravel dust cloud.

Take that, demolition people.

The trucks are already there, evil bulldozer poised and rumbling. The men are at their machines, annoyed at our entrance, sipping coffee, waiting for a signal. A few of them look at us curiously, but I just wave at them and ride around to the dock. What are they going to tell us? That we can't watch? I have seniority here.

Rock follows suit and steps out of his car, his feet crunching over the gravel. I'll miss that sound. "What are they going to build here?" He squints against the sun.

"Probably some ridiculously big house with no love in it."

"Maybe it'll be a perfectly modest house with a nice family in it."

"Whatever," I grunt.

"Maybe," he says, sitting down and pulling me with him, "we'll live in it one day." The wooden planks are already warm this early in the day. It's going to be a hot summer.

"Don't even say that. It'll never happen, and you're making me sad."

He wraps his arm around my shoulders and pulls me into him.

"They're kicking me out of my place, Rock. No likey."

"I know. But you'll find a new place," he says, just as a man in a hard hat gives the others a signal.

I bury my face in Rock's neck and brace myself. I could never have done this by myself. Even with my constants around me—sun, moon, hundred billion stars in this galaxy alone—I need Rock in my universe.

He gives my cheek a few feathery kisses in an attempt to distract me. *It's okay*, I tell myself. *I'm ready to let go*. Two seconds later, the evil bulldozer lunges into action, miserably rolls forward, and chomps right down into the Murphys' living room.

Acknowledgments

With unwavering gratitude and love, I thank the following people for their support during this unpredictable ride—Noah and Murphy, for being good babies who let me write *Riding the Universe* in five-minute spurts during their first year; Michael, for the interest to always ask which scene I wrote that day; my stepdaughter, Devin, for her intelligent suggestions; my colleagues, Danielle Joseph, Adrienne Sylver, Linda Rodriguez Bernfeld, and Marjetta Geerling, for reading early drafts and providing excellent feedback; my amazing agent, Steven Chudney, for going along with my ideas and being the best agent ever—period; my editor, Sarah Sevier, for her incredible insight and patience; and finally my husband, Chris Nuñez, for coaxing Motor Girl out of me and onto the page, for believing in me always, and for telling me to write, baby, write, because that's what writers do. I love you.